PUF

EVEN MOR

When the *offensive* Julia Channing is pronounced a 'gifted child' and then appointed Monitor of the Band Room at Lord Willoughby's (the school's 'Junior Leisure and Recreation Centre'), her tyrannical reign goads Annabel into retaliation. Inspired by a story in an old comic she has seen the Deputy Head, Mrs da Susa, reading, she enlists the help of Kate and Sheena and they don masks, robes and hoods to become the Silent Three, fighting tyranny and injustice – with outrageously funny consequences.

The second of these two stories sees Annabel campaigning for the rotten things of life (in particular, the decaying old tree in Addendon Rec) and in doing so becoming the unwitting focus of a live television programme and turning up rather more dead wood than she'd anticipated.

Even More Like Annabel is brimming with all the invention and humour that have made Annabel such a memorable character.

Also published in Puffin are a *Friend Like Annabel*, *Just Like Annabel* and *The New, Thinking Annabel*. Married with four children and living in Dorset, Alan Davidson is also the author of the marvellously gripping *The Bewitching of Alison Allbright*.

Other books by Alan Davidson

A FRIEND LIKE ANNABEL
JUST LIKE ANNABEL
THE NEW, THINKING ANNABEL
LITTLE YEARNINGS OF ANNABEL

THE BEWITCHING OF ALISON ALLBRIGHT

ALAN DAVIDSON

*****

Even more like
Annabel

PUFFIN BOOKS

PUFFIN BOOKS

Published by the Penguin Group
27 Wrights Lane, London w 8 5 tz, England
Viking Penguin Inc., 40 West 23rd Street, New York, New York 10010, USA
Penguin Books Australia Ltd, Ringwood, Victoria, Australia
Penguin Books Canada Ltd, 2801 John Street, Markham, Ontario, Canada L 3 R 1 B 4
Penguin Books (NZ) Ltd, 182–190 Wairau Road, Auckland 10, New Zealand

Penguin Books Ltd, Registered Offices: Harmondsworth, Middlesex, England

First published by Granada Publishing 1985
Published in Puffin Books 1989
1 3 5 7 9 10 8 6 4 2

Made and printed in Great Britain by
Hazell, Watson and Viney Ltd, Member of BPCC, Aylesbury, Bucks.
Filmset in Linotron 202 Trump Medieval by
Rowland Phototypesetting Ltd, Bury St Edmunds, Suffolk

To Tessa's friend Vikki

Contents

*****

Annabel and the coming of the
   Silent Three to Lord Willoughby's   9

Annabel and the rotten things of life   103

Annabel
and the coming of the
Silent Three to
Lord Willoughby's

*****

Chapter 1

✳✳✳✳✳

In an underground room, lit only by a guttering candle flame which cast moving shadows upon the barred windows and mysterious shelved recesses, three cloaked, hooded and masked figures sat at a small box-like table with a black cloth thrown over it. Above their masks, each bore a number daubed in white upon the grey of the hood and a sharp-eyed observer might have noticed that for some reason, possibly connected with the dark machinations of sorcery, the number 3 was upside down.

One of the three was writing carefully, in block capitals, upon a plain square of thick white paper. Even without the *1* on her hood she (for it *was* a she) would have been recognizable as the leader from the aura of quiet authority which somehow surrounded her.

Having finished her writing, she slid the piece of paper across the black cloth to the hooded figure on her right.

'What do you think of that, Number Two?' she asked, quietly.

Number Two gazed at the piece of paper and nodded slowly.

'Shouldn't it be *have*?' she asked, 'rather than *has*?'

'No,' replied Number One. 'We are a collective

noun. If you are otherwise satisfied, Number Two, please pass it to Number Three.'

Number Three fumbled with her mask as the paper was pushed in front of her.

'Well, Number Three,' said Number One, after a pause, 'do you agree upon the wording?'

Number Three tittered nervously and continued to fumble.

'I'm awfully sorry, Number One, but I can't see it. I can't find the eye-holes.'

'Then adjust your mask, Number Three,' said Number One, sharply. 'It's nearly round the side of your head.'

Number Three tittered again, this time feebly. 'I'm afraid the elastic's going,' she said apologetically. She lifted the mask and squinted underneath.

'I think that's splendid.'

'Then we are agreed,' said Number One. She held out her hand for the paper to be returned to her. The wording on it read:

THIS IS YOUR FINAL WARNING, JULIA CHANNING!
THE DAYS OF YOUR EVIL TYRANNY ARE
NUMBERED! THE SILENT THREE
HAS MARKED YOU DOWN AND JUSTICE WILL ONCE
AGAIN REIGN AT LORD WILLOUGHBY'S

'Now I think it must be supper-time,' said Number One. 'I'm getting hungry.'

'So am I, Annabel,' sighed Number Two.

For the leader of this strange and dedicated organization, meeting secretly somewhere in Lord Willoughby's School, Addendon, long after everyone else had gone home, was Annabel Fidelity Bunce of Class 3 G.

★

To discover why the Silent Three had to step out of the pages of an old comic to haunt Lord Willoughby's School and seek justice for the oppressed, it is necessary to go back a few days; to the Thursday, to be precise, on which Annabel Bunce quarrelled with Julia Channing in the Old Band Room during dinner break.

The Old Band Room is a square, thatched, whitewashed building standing by itself in the school grounds at some distance from the main block. It had been acquired by the school in passing, as it were, a few years earlier when they had bought the land on which it stood for extensions to the grounds and playing fields. The Addendon Silver Band, whose Headquarters it had formerly been, had parted with it most happily for the price they had received and marched off to new, less draughty premises in Gamble Street leaving the school wondering what to do with it.

Mrs da Susa, the Deputy Head, then quite newly appointed and even more full of reforming zeal than she was now, had decided that it should be a place to which the younger pupils, Third Year and under, could retreat at break-times away from, as she put it, 'the pressures of school life' and play games or make things or otherwise express themselves in ways chosen by themselves. She had had it furnished with tables and chairs, armchairs, a table tennis table and other games and named it *The Junior Leisure and Recreation Centre* though nobody bothered with that and it was always referred to simply as 'the Old Band Room', or, more simply still, 'the Band Room'.

Above all she had hoped that it would be made use of by the more underprivileged pupils whose home conditions didn't allow them to express themselves there.

On this particular day, it being wet outside, the Band Room was crowded with juniors playing games and expressing themselves in various ways, some of them not anticipated by Mrs da Susa.

Annabel was there with her best friend Kate Stocks. They were helping Sheena Franks-Walters to master table tennis though why she wanted to do so was puzzling them for she didn't even seem very interested in it. Sheena, 3 G's only wealthy, well-bred member, normally kept herself remote from school activities and Annabel and Kate, with whom she had a special relationship, were her only confidantes.

She had asked them about the table tennis that morning saying she wanted to make herself good at it for a special reason but she hadn't elaborated and, as Annabel remarked to Kate, it was to be hoped it wasn't urgent. She was inclined to go off into a little daydream after making a stroke, so that even if she did succeed in keeping one of her high-bouncing serves on the table she might be gazing benignly into space by the time it came back to her.

Annabel, dancing round in her socks, tried to keep her awake by hitting the ball straight to her as often

14

as possible while Kate stood patiently by her to field any missed ones.

Other games were being played at tables or on the floor, variously involving cards or the tossing or flicking of coins. The voices of Richard White and Damian Price, both of 3G, could be heard frequently, raised in heated argument. At a table in a dark corner a First Year boy sat alone, facing the wall, bent over something, a tiny island of quiet and concentration in a sea of din.

Towards this carefree scene, however, a cloud was drifting in the shape of Julia Channing, the *offensive* Julia Channing as Annabel was accustomed to call her when in charitable mood. Her dark permed hair bounced importantly as she walked.

She had been looking particularly full of herself for the last day or two and Annabel had remarked upon it. It was as if she were hugging some secret she was bursting to reveal if only someone would ask her what it was. Annabel and Kate had taken good care not to, of course.

Entering the Band Room, Julia went to one of the armchairs and pushed it over to the window, just behind Annabel. Annabel observed this without taking her eye off the ball, which she was tapping back to Sheena.

'You can't sit there, Julia,' she said, patiently. 'You're in the way.'

'It's you that's in the way,' replied Julia, sitting down. 'This is the only place where it's light enough to read my newspaper.'

Julia reading a newspaper! This was strange. It

was well known that she hadn't yet graduated from the *Beano* to more mature comics. Still, that was Julia's silly business. Table tennis was, for the moment, Annabel's. Sheena, having hit the ball under the table, was disappearing laboriously in search of it and Annabel turned round.

'I have to warn you,' she said, still patient, 'that if you are going to sit there neither I, nor Kate, nor possibly even Sheena, will be responsible for the consequences. This is table tennis space.'

Kate firmly nodded her agreement and Sheena, crawling out from under the table, did the same, a frown on her normally sweet face. This might ordinarily have had some effect since Julia usually toadied to Sheena, but on this occasion she seemed beyond caring. She merely spread her newspaper widely in front of her.

It was *The Times*.

This was so extraordinary that Annabel and Kate quite forgot their grievances for a moment. But only for a moment. Obviously, this was merely a Julia-ism. She would certainly not be doing any reading behind there, though she might possibly have found something to interest her: an animal picture, perhaps, or some simple cartoon which she could frown over and try to get the point of.

She was showing off. For some reason she was attempting to demonstrate to everyone that she was now a *Times* reader. Though all she was actually doing was setting teeth on edge.

'Your serve, Sheena,' snapped Annabel, her patience wearing thin.

Sheena's service was one of her tentative, high-bouncing ones but even so, in stepping back to receive it, Annabel trod on Julia's foot. Julia leapt to her feet.

'This is impossible,' she cried. 'Here I am, trying to read my *Times* and you won't let me, fooling around with that mindless game. That table ought to be somewhere where it doesn't interfere with people who are trying to do more intelligent things. Move it over there!'

She pointed imperiously to the ill-lit and cramped recess on the other side of the room, at present occupied by some Second Year boys scuffling around on their knees playing a game which involved rolling coins.

The look in Annabel's eyes persuaded her to drop her arm. Nevertheless she plonked herself stubbornly down in the armchair again and flung *The Times* open still wider than before.

'Kate,' said Annabel, now in a rage, 'why don't you demonstrate some smashes to Sheena. I'll send up some easy ones.'

Kate, no less enraged, obligingly directed a smash straight at Julia's head and Annabel, leaping for it with furious energy, managed to swipe *The Times* aside with her bat. The ball hit Julia on the nose.

'You hooligans,' screamed Julia, leaping up again. 'You've torn my *Times*.'

'It's not your *Times*,' panted Annabel. 'It's somebody called Mr Speedley's. His name's written on the corner. Anyway, it's yesterday's. You found it in a litter bin.'

She thumped her bat down on the table and for a moment the situation looked dangerous. Cries of 'shut up' and similar came from other quarters of the Band Room.

Julia looked from Annabel's face to Kate's and then to Sheena's and admitted defeat. Normally at this stage she would have flounced off in a sulk but instead, although she paled a little, she actually calmed down. She seemed to have found a new source of inner strength from somewhere. She had the look of someone with a devastating counter-blow at her disposal who was hesitating to use it out of kindness. Then she set these scruples aside.

'I'm gifted,' she announced, casually but vengefully, starting to fold up the newspaper. 'You're not.'

'Gifted?' echoed Kate, coming to join Annabel. 'Gifted at what?'

'Everything,' said Julia. 'I was born a gifted child. I've got an exceptionally high IQ. People like you drag me back.'

So this was what she'd been striving to convey; this the secret she had been hugging. It wasn't very interesting after all. Just some new fantasy of hers; or, more likely, her mother's.

'Then why aren't you coming top in everything?' inquired Kate, nastily.

'I told you. My environment's against me,' said Julia, carefully placing the folded up *Times* under one arm. 'Thick people like you. I ought really to be at a special school.'

Annabel snorted and muttered a suggestion as to which, turning her back on Julia. 'We'd better pack this in anyway,' she said to Kate and Sheena. 'It's R.E. in five minutes.'

The Band Room was starting to empty as Lord Willoughby's prepared itself for afternoon school.

'It's not going to go on like this, though,' cried Julia, becoming belligerent again at being ignored. 'Something's going to be done about it.'

Annabel made a further suggestion under her breath and started taking the table tennis net down. 'You go on,' she said to Sheena. 'Kate and I'll put the stuff away. Anyway I've still got to put my shoes on.' This was said because Sheena always padded along at such an unhurryable pace that she would need to start out now to get to R.E. in time and not hold up the others.

Kate took the bats and ball into the store-room where they were kept and Annabel went in after her with the net. Julia, still aggressive, tried to follow.

'My mum's coming to see Mrs da Susa about it this afternoon,' she hooted. Annabel closed the door on her.

'You'll see,' she could be heard calling outside the door as they put the equipment away on a shelf, but they paid no attention. With luck she'd have gone when they emerged. As for her mother, if she really were coming to Willers to make absurd claims then Mrs da Susa would know how to show her the door. Everyone had their limits, even Mrs da Susa.

Closing the door of the store-room turned out to have been a mistake, for when Annabel opened it again it was to see Julia hurling her shoes – which she had removed to play table tennis – out of the

Band Room, one after the other, in the direction of some clumps of bamboo and then fleeing in the opposite direction. Once more enraged, Annabel had to search for the shoes in her socks, in the rain, helped by a sympathetic Kate and by Mr Toogood, their English teacher who had happened to notice the shoes flying through the air while passing and had come over to see what was happening.

Mr Toogood inflamed Annabel the more by implying that he held her and Kate responsible for the 'horseplay' as he called it. He hadn't actually seen who'd thrown the shoes and they couldn't tell him since they did have their principles, even where Julia was concerned. He wasn't even any help in finding the shoes, Annabel herself finding the first and Kate the second.

By the time they were on their way to R.E., Annabel was in a state of fury with Julia in particular and Lord Willoughby's in general. It was all too typical, she explained to Kate, of the daily round of injustices and tyrannies that made up life at Willers. If only they didn't have to get to R.E. in a hurry she'd have loved to have reminded Kate of just some of the things that had happened during the last few days. This was only one example, although certainly Julia was in a class of her own when it came to being repellent, offensive not, upon consideration, being nearly a strong enough word for her. Just imagine Julia actually having any power over anybody! Imagine it! But one day, she assured Kate, Willers *and* Julia would go too far.

What would happen then she didn't have time to

explain because at that point they arrived at the classroom door and had to brace themselves for yet more unpleasantness, being ten minutes late for R.E.

But it didn't happen. On the contrary, what was to happen was to put Annabel back into a thoroughly good mood, at any rate temporarily. As she opened the door and led the way into the classroom she immediately saw that there was something wrong with the scene that confronted her.

3G themselves looked ordinary enough. They were bent over their desks copying out a map of the Holy Land from the blackboard. There were a few exceptions. Julia was looking at them out of the corner of her eye, her expression a blend of triumph and nervousness. Miles Noggins was on the point of nodding off to sleep, mouth open and elbow about to slip off the desk; Damian Price was hitting Ben Ramsay repeatedly on the back of the head with a pencil and sniggering under his breath at the other's attempts to catch his hand; Sheena Franks-Walters was as usual gazing sweetly into space, her face clouded by a slight frown. On the whole, though, it was a reasonable picture of industry and concentration.

In contrast, Mrs da Susa was reading a comic under the desk. She was resting it on her knees where it was discreetly hidden from the class, and she was so engrossed in it that it was a moment or two before she was aware of Annabel and Kate's presence. Annabel could tell it was a comic because she could see the picture strips.

It was the wrong way round as Mrs da Susa was evidently quick to appreciate, for as soon as she did realize that Annabel and Kate were standing staring at her she started guiltily and in some confusion closed the comic and dropped it on to what appeared to be a stack of similar comics under the knee-hole of her desk.

'Er – you're late,' she said.

'Yes, Mrs da Susa,' agreed Annabel.

'You'd – er – better sit down. The others are copying out a map of the Holy Land.'

That was all. It was feeble. Even the map of the Holy Land was suspicious, Mrs da Susa normally preferring the sound of her own voice in R.E. on subjects considerably trendier than that of the Holy Land. It smacked of keeping the class quiet while she read her comic.

It was intriguing and, as Annabel whispered to Kate as they sat down, 'It must be a pretty good comic and I'm dying to see what it is.'

The opportunity came at the end of the lesson when Mrs da Susa gathered her books and departed quickly as if to keep an appointment elsewhere and, whether absent-mindedly or by design, left the comics where they were.

3G's next lesson was Chemistry and Julia Channing left the room quickly too, almost treading on Mrs da Susa's heels and casting apprehensive glances back at Annabel. For the moment, however, Annabel was more interested in the comics and as soon as the room was empty save for her and Kate, she investigated.

'It's not a modern comic,' she said, picking up the top one which Mrs da Susa had been reading. 'Look, Kate, it's an old one.'

'They all are,' said Kate, getting down on one knee and riffling through the others. 'It's a file of them, all in order. I wonder if they were Mrs da Susa's comics when she was our age?' That was an intriguing thought.

'They look better than modern comics,' said Annabel, turning over the pages. 'Look at this story, Kate: the Silent Three at St Babs. It looks really good. It's about three girls at a smart public school who dress themselves up in robes and masks to fight the injustices of a tyrannical prefect.' Annabel shuddered with pleasure at the sound of it. 'Oh, and look Kate, look! There's the tyrannical prefect. Who does she remind you of?'

Annabel's voice had become gleeful and she pointed to one of the drawings.

'Julia!' cried Kate at once. 'Julia Channing!'

The likeness really was remarkable.

'Julia with speech balloons! Oh, Kate, their villainess looked just like our villainess. Now I *know* it's a good story. It's got its finger on the pulse. Kate, I must have a quick read. We've got a few minutes before Chemmy.'

It had put Annabel back into a great good humour. It didn't occur to her, or to Kate, that this might be a portent, that the long shadow of St Babs might be about to cast itself over Lord Willoughby's.

Chapter 2

✳✳✳✳✳

Mrs da Susa, Deputy Head of Lord Willoughby's School, had discovered the comics on the previous evening. At about ten o'clock she had found herself, unusually for her, at a loose end having done her day's work at school, marked some homework, completed her notes for the Fifth Year's English lesson on the following day, made supper for Mr da Susa and herself and unblocked the outflow of the washing machine which had been giving trouble. Now she had an hour or two to fill before retiring to bed.

She made to go into the sitting-room intending to ask her husband if he would like a game of Scrabble or Newmarket, then remembered that he'd gone out after supper and still wasn't back. She'd had to speak to him quite sharply recently about making a mess in the house with a lot of wood shavings and sawdust and she suspected that he was deliberately leaving her alone in the evenings because he was sulking. Mr da Susa, who had been happily unemployed for some years, had been making a model ship or something. It was his latest hobby.

Instead, she wandered into her tiny den where she had her desk and files. Perhaps this would be a good opportunity to tidy up her cupboard, which she had been long meaning to do. She'd quite forgotten what was in it.

The bottom part of the cupboard was crammed with items of interest that, sentimental old thing that she was, she had hoarded over the years: old newspapers, photographs, theatre programmes, her childhood stamp album. At the bottom of the stack she was momentarily surprised to come across a pile of magazines carefully filed in a cardboard cover. Then realization dawned and her face softened. Her old comics! Lovingly saved from all those years ago!

Nothing could have brought back her girlhood more vividly: the large Edwardian house in North London – her father had been a senior civil servant – and, even more, the small, expensive, incompetent private school in East Anglia where she had been educated.

She hadn't had any friends there but that hadn't bothered her. She had been a worker amongst debbie-type drones forever gossiping about clothes and make-up. No, Mrs da Susa, or Muriel Pipps as she had then been (how thrilled she had been to marry her Italian husband and exchange her maiden name for what she saw as the glamorous 'da Susa'!) had had no need of them. She had had a truer, more reliable friend: this comic. Most days after finishing her prep she would retire to the privacy of the dormitory with an apple and, eyes popping, settle down to browse through the serial stories. And – yes – here was her favourite, The Silent Three at St Babs! What memories that brought back! She got an apple from the bowl for old time's sake and settled down for a read.

It was about three fourth-formers at a girls' public school who had banded together to form the Silent Three. Wearing, when necessary, masks and robes and vowed to secrecy, their purpose had been to end the harsh rule of a tyrannical prefect called Mavis. Besides being a tyrant, Mavis was playing what was described as a 'deep game' about something which Mrs da Susa had forgotten, but which appeared to be – so she understood as she became immersed in the story again – to do with a hoard of jewels hidden in the school grounds by a criminal who was now serving a life sentence for stealing them. Mavis's activities led to a great injustice when a first-former was falsely accused of misdeeds which were not actually hers and threatened with expulsion. Helping Mavis and trying to thwart the Silent Three, for no better reason than that she enjoyed sneaking, was the Form Sneak, Freda.

Mrs da Susa pored over the story. Despite a number of holes and inconsistencies – why, for example, did the Silent Three always insist upon donning their robes and masks at moments when they wished to remain incognito, when that seemed to be the surest way of drawing attention to themselves? – it still made compulsive reading. But what worried her now was the story's *outlook* on life. How greatly attitudes had changed – for the better, of course – since she was at school!

It was clear to her now, for example, that Mavis must be in need of the sort of sympathy and understanding from her Headmistress which she had simply not been getting. Surely she was merely reacting to the pressures upon her which must have been enormous! And Freda! What had turned her into the sort of girl she was? It wasn't enough merely to brand them as tyrant and sneak respectively. They had to be understood.

Mrs da Susa took a second apple and ruminated. She hoped that now she was a Head – or rather, and there was a slight darkening of the brow, a *Deputy* Head – she would know how to deal sympathetically with a Mavis or a Freda. Surely, however, there were lessons here for the modern girl and the modern boy, too. It might be an interesting exercise to discuss the moral issues brought up by the story during an R.E. lesson. It would make a change from nuclear disarmament.

She was prevented from finishing the serial that evening by the return of Mr da Susa wanting his cocoa – apparently he'd been on a long walk which he must have enjoyed very much for he seemed very stimulated – but the thought appealed to her which was why she had brought the comics to the R.E. lesson. She was trying to finish the story when interrupted by Annabel and Kate, an event which caused her some embarrassment; quite unnecessarily of course for she was only reading the comic for research, but nevertheless it must have looked rather odd and she decided to leave the discussion till another time.

At the end of the lesson she left the comics under her desk to be collected later, being in a hurry to get away because she had an appointment with Julia Channing's mother who wanted to see her on a matter, apparently, of some urgency.

Proceeding to her study to keep the appointment Mrs da Susa suddenly realized who it was that Mavis, the villainess of the picture story, reminded her of so strongly.

Of course! She was the image of Julia Channing.

*

'This Mavis is a real creepie,' murmured Annabel. 'She's almost as bad as the real Julia.'

'I can't wait to see her bowled out,' said Kate. 'Letting that poor little first-former be blamed and told she's going to be expelled! I hope she gets what she deserves.'

'It's an injustice,' agreed Annabel, vehemently, 'a great injustice. Have you finished that page, Kate?'

They were flicking through the comics at breakneck speed, trying to read as much as possible before they had to go to Chemistry.

'Still,' said Kate, opening up the next comic, 'it's obvious that Mavis is just a pathetic pawn in the whole thing. She's being used by this mystery man who keeps appearing and his accomplice in the school, whoever that is.'

'That's Julia all over,' said Annabel, contemptuously. 'There's the bell, Kate. Better go in a minute. Just time for one more instalment.'

'I wonder if they'll still be here after school,' said Kate, who was as wrapped up in the story as Annabel.

'We could look back and see.'

Reluctantly they tore themselves away from Mavis, the Great Injustice, the Deep Game and the Silent Three.

★

'So nice to see you, Mrs Channing,' said Mrs da Susa as her visitor took the proffered seat. Julia's mother was dressed in a bright pink blouse which, together with her bright blond hair and white skirt, made her look like an ice-cream.

'How are you, Mrs da Susa?' she said. 'I think I've found the answer. I only hope I've found it in time, though late in the day is better than never. I do think, though, that it's unfortunate it hasn't been realized before and it seems a pity that it has been left to a non-expert like myself when surely it should have been picked up by those trained to have the expertise –'

It occurred to Mrs da Susa that Mrs Channing was not still referring to how she, Mrs da Susa, was. 'Excuse me,' she interrupted, cautiously, 'the answer to what?'

'The answer, of course,' said Mrs Channing, puzzled by the question, 'to why my Julia only came twenty-seventh in term order, of course. Last time it was twenty-fourth and the time before twenty-fifth and it's obvious that for a girl of her abilities there's something wrong, I think we're all agreed on that, but it wasn't till I saw this programme on telly that it hit me. Julia's a gifted child and such children need special treatment if they're to realize their proper potential. It's obvious isn't it. They told you

29

the points to watch for.' Mrs Channing ticked them off on her fingers. 'They don't need much sleep when they're little, they get very curious about things, they're easily bored and they've got minds that keep jumping from one thing to another, and they often get on badly with their peer group which I think means the other people in their class. Now I'm not sure about this sleep business, I can't remember, but all the other things are Julia exactly and it's just a pity that wasn't realized when she was seven or eight years old because if it had been and Julia had been given the special treatment a gifted child has a right to expect, then it would all have been very different. I shall always blame myself in a way, though why I should be expected to recognize it when other highly trained people haven't I'm not sure.' She shot a mildly reproachful glance at Mrs da Susa. 'I don't want to be critical but I do think Mr Trimm's a little bit out of touch, which is why I came to you.'

This reference to the Headmaster of Lord Willoughby's was designed to warm Mrs da Susa's heart. However, she continued to look cautious. It was true that Julia was butterfly-minded, nosey and unpopular but . . .

'In what way is she inquisitive about things?' she asked. 'How does she spend her free time?'

'Ballet on Tuesdays and yoghurt – silly me, I mean yoga – on Fridays. The rest of the time she watches telly. We've given her a telly and video of her own to put in her den. She just closes the door in the evenings and that's it. She's insatiable.'

'You mean she's watching educational programmes?' asked Mrs da Susa, frowning as she tried to recall the frequency of educational programmes on evening television.

'It's all education, isn't it? It's a window on the world. Julia has to get her education in this way because she's lonely. It's like what the programme said. All gifted children are lonely unless they've got others of the same intellect as themselves around them to discuss things with. And that's what Julia lacks, you see. Maybe, there's nobody at Lord Willoughby's who's really suitable as a friend for her but at least she ought to be consorting with the top people in her class like that Deborah Breakspear and Julian Parlane instead of people like – like Tracey Cooke and' – Mrs Channing cast around for the most telling example she could think of – 'that Annabel Bunce.'

'She's lonely, is she?' asked Mrs da Susa, grasping at the one element in the situation in which she could see a remote possibility of taking action.

'Hungry for intellectual company is the way I'd put it,' said Mrs Channing.

That way of putting it made the whole thing sound impossible again unless Julia were to be removed from Lord Willoughby's altogether.

'I'll give the matter deep thought,' sighed Mrs da Susa.

★

'So the biggest crook of all was the Headmistress herself!' said Annabel with a pleasurable shudder.

'The dignified Miss Sterndale! *She* was the mysterious accomplice. Amazing!'

It was now late afternoon. School was over and every other pupil of Lord Willoughby's had gone home – save for a few in detention – but Annabel and Kate were still in the classroom finishing off the Silent Three serial, Mrs da Susa not having taken her comics away yet.

'And the mystery man was her brother, a ne'er-do-well who'd broken out of gaol to search for a hoard of jewels buried in the school grounds. He'd learned about it from a fellow prisoner who'd stolen the stuff and concealed it there. Phew!'

'A pretty deep game all right,' murmured Kate. 'Miss Sterndale only applied for the job as Head in the first place because her brother wanted her to look for the loot. And when she couldn't find it he had to come himself. As for Mavis, she was just a stupid but useful pawn!'

Annabel closed the last comic and arranged it tidily on the pile. 'I bet not many people at St Babs passed any exams with all that going on,' she sighed. 'Marvellous story, though!'

The rattle of the cleaners' buckets could be heard outside and they left. As they walked home along Church Lane they were still reflecting on the story. On Annabel in particular it had made a deep impression.

'Mavis got off lightly if you ask me,' she said, 'just being thrown in the school swimming-pool. So did Freda come to that. They'll be tyrannizing and sneaking again given half a chance. They can't seem to stop it.'

She brooded.

'It was good to see the Silent Three winning through in the end, though, wasn't it, Kate? At least virtue triumphed at St Babs which is more than it ever does at Willers. Perhaps,' she added reflectively, 'we need a Silent Three here. There are plenty of injustices to put right. It's just one after another.'

This led Annabel to summarize some of the more recent ones, as many as she had time for before they had to separate.

Only that morning, for instance, Annabel had been awarded a C- for her history homework by Mrs Jesty while Naomi Peach had got a B+. The monstrous injustice of this was that it had been the *same homework*, originally done by Annabel and subsequently hastily copied out by Naomi who had come into the classroom panic-stricken only minutes before the homework was due to be handed in and begging for someone's to crib because she had been ill on the evening before, or so she claimed. Generously, Annabel had lent her hers and such had been her bitter reward. Annabel had really tried hard with that homework, too, while Naomi's had been a hurried scribble with bits missed out. What did St Babs know of injustice?

Annabel was carrying on in this vein when they found themselves at the corner of Badger's Close, where she lived.

'Well,' sighed Kate, as they were about to part, 'I

suppose the only thing you can say about Willers is that at least Mrs da Susa isn't a crook with a gaolbird for a brother and Julia isn't a prefect with any power over us.'

Annabel considered that.

'I prefer to keep an open mind,' she said. 'At Willers, anything's possible. If not now, in the future.'

They were prophetic words. At that moment Mrs da Susa was collecting the comics. She was particularly interested now in having another look at the Silent Three story.

*

She studied it again at home that evening. It now seemed to her significant that she should have come across the story just as Mrs Channing was about to see her; particularly significant that Mavis was the image of Julia. Surely it must have been sent as a sign.

Without it, she might have succumbed to the temptation simply to try to keep out of Mrs Channing's way for a time, though certainly that would have been difficult for, in Julia's interests, Mrs Channing would be formidable and persistent. Unless satisfied she would do her best to make Mrs da Susa's life a misery, telephoning at inopportune moments, delivering unstoppable monologues at parents' evenings, lurking in wait to accost her.

The Silent Three story had come as a firm reminder of where her duty lay; to warn her against failing with Julia as the short-sighted and outdated Miss Sterndale had failed with Mavis.

(True, having now finished the story, she recalled that Miss Sterndale had had other things on her mind but the parts about the gaolbird brother and so on were merely there for dramatic effect and not to be taken seriously as an integral part of the story. Having studied English at Oxford Mrs da Susa did, after all, have a sharply analytical eye for a story and was well able to tell what an author was trying to say, even when that author didn't know it him- or herself.)

But what could she do for Julia? On the face of it there seemed little. Obviously, in watching the programme about gifted children Mrs Channing had filtered the information in her mind, seizing upon what she wanted to hear and allowing the rest to pass over her head.

However, there must be *something*. Others might dismiss Julia as merely a pain in the neck but she, Mrs da Susa, with her training and experience, knew better. It was simply a question of finding the key which would unlock the talents and virtues which certainly lay hidden there; which lay hidden in everyone.

Perhaps what Julia needed was a *role* in the school . . . to be given an *identity* . . . something which would stretch her and bring out those latent qualities . . .

Mrs da Susa had received a note from Mr Trimm that afternoon. Recalling it now, she fished it out of her brief-case. It was asking if she might kindly do something about indiscipline in the Band Room. The Junior Leisure and Recreation Centre had, after all, been her idea.

She ignored the touch of asperity in the last sentence. She was used to that from Mr Trimm. Studying the note again, she brightened.

*

The news broke in Assembly the following morning. Annabel and Kate were sitting behind Julia and they could see from her attitude that she was anticipating something of interest. She was looking unusually alert, sitting bolt upright and listening expectantly. Suddenly they noticed that her ears had turned bright red and then the back of her neck proceeded to do the same.

Mr Trimm had brought up the subject of the Band Room. Crouched ponderously over his lectern he was booming about the unsatisfactoriness of the present arrangements. The Band Room was being used inconsiderately and for purposes inconsistent with its original ideals (he blenched and scowled slightly when he said this and it was to be assumed that someone else had written it for him). Moreover, there was persistent horseplay there. Only yesterday a master had observed a pair of shoes being hurled out of the door (Annabel nudged Kate and nodded with satisfaction). This sort of behaviour had to stop (another satisfied nudge).

Accordingly he had decided to appoint a Band Room Monitor whose duties would be to revitalize it, ensure its smooth running and maintain a proper discipline there. As Monitor he had chosen (his tone became disbelieving) Julia Channing of Class 3 G. She would be in charge of all matters to do with the Band Room and her instructions in respect of it were to be obeyed.

At this Julia's ears flamed again and she half rose, looking about her excitedly as if expecting applause, while Annabel's mouth fell open. Mr Trimm appeared to snort and mutter to himself before tossing the paper aside and moving on to the next announcement.

Mrs da Susa meanwhile was nodding approvingly. She had acted decisively, having decided that an appointment such as this was exactly what was required to stimulate and challenge Julia and bring her into the mainstream of school life. She had composed the announcement for Mr Trimm on the previous evening and informed Julia just before Assembly. Yes, *this* decidedly was the way Miss Sterndale ought to have handled Mavis.

3 G greeted the news somewhat differently, their reactions probably being best summarized by Richard White's throaty guffaw.

As for Annabel, her mouth remained open.

What did St Babs know of injustice when compared with Lord Willoughby's? Their Headmistress had been a comparatively harmless crook with another comparatively harmless crook for a brother. Their actions had been, in the particular circumstances, reasonably logical and intelligible.

'Oh, Kate, they've actually given Julia *power*! There'll be a reign of terror. It'll be just like Mavis.'

Chapter 3

*****

Julia had entered Assembly as plain, ordinary Julia Channing. She emerged Julia Channing, Band Room Monitor, taller, straighter, brighter of eye and, to Annabel's mind, doubly insufferable.

Most of 3 G was standing around in groups outside the hall discussing the announcement when she made her exit, having apparently delayed it to gain maximum effect and hold a press conference. She paused briefly by Annabel and Kate who were just leaving a group.

'I told you I was gifted,' she announced. 'You didn't believe me, did you, but I expect you're sorry about that now. It's because I'm gifted that I've been selected for this appointment. Never before, in the history of Lord Willoughby's, has anyone from the Third Year been given such an important post. So that just shows you, doesn't it.' She laughed excitedly. She was shaking a little.

Annabel rolled her eyes.

'I hope,' said Kate bitterly, 'that since you're Band Room Monitor now you'll launch an urgent investigation into which hooligan it was that threw those shoes out of the Band Room. We can't have that sort of behaviour in your Band Room, can we?'

'I expect whoever it was was acting under provocation,' said Julia and she laughed again, moving on.

'She's on a high,' muttered Annabel. 'You can't reason with her now, even if you ever could.'

Julia paused and looked round, having half-heard. 'Did you say something about me?' she inquired. 'I should be careful if I were you. I'm a Monitor now and a Monitor's words carry special weight, even in connection with things other than their immediate responsibilities. It's like being a Cabinet Minister.' There was a bounce in her step as she proceeded, to be halted again by Mrs da Susa calling her from the Hall doorway.

'Julia, would you care to come to my office now and collect the keys to the Band Room.'

'Certainly, Mrs da Susa,' replied Julia, airily, as one leading figure in the school to another. She went bouncing off in Mrs da Susa's wake.

'Unbelievable!' said Annabel. 'Even for Willers!' She seemed uncharacteristically dazed as they made their way towards Geography.

'Perhaps,' said Kate, 'we should boycott the Band Room while Julia's in charge.'

That brought Annabel out of her daze.

'Certainly *not*, Kate. Julia's not going to drive *me* away from there. *Band Room Monitor!* Ugh! I mean to go in there on principle! Even when I don't *want* to! Today! At dinner break!'

*

Watching Julia leave her study with the Band Room keys, Mrs da Susa experienced a glow of satisfaction. She had noticed the spring in Julia's step and was pleased.

'As I hoped,' she thought, 'this has given her a new lease of life, a new purpose.'

She had handed over the two large old keys, one to the Band Room door itself, the other to the store-room, stressing to Julia that she must take great care not to lose them for at present the only spares had been mislaid.

She had also drawn Julia's attention – if a little dubiously – to the Junior Chess Club which met on Saturday mornings at ten. Its membership at present was limited to Julian Parlane of the Third Year and one First Year boy so it was in need of new talent, and in view of what her mother had said it would seem desirable that Julia should join. (Mrs da Susa's main motive in this, it must be admitted, was to make sure that Mrs Channing would be unable to accuse her of not trying.)

Julia had replied that perhaps it was a pity that First Years were allowed in because it didn't give them much of a chance and made it less fun for the older ones, but nevertheless she'd be delighted to give it a try; a reply which Mrs da Susa welcomed as a sign of growing confidence.

Yes, she thought, this was the real joy of being a Head – or, rather, Deputy Head. To help shape and guide a personality and subtly bring out the best in one's pupils. Under her discreet guidance, Julia would not be a Mavis.

'Julia,' muttered Annabel meanwhile as she settled down for Geography, 'is a pain in the neck. I'd like to throw her in the swimming pool.'

It was a clear difference of opinion, not for the first time, between Annabel and Mrs da Susa.

*

Annabel and Kate presented themselves at the Band Room at dinner break as soon as they'd eaten their sandwiches. Julia was already there, having forgone dinner in her excitement. Some First Year boys and girls were just leaving, carrying between them cleaning materials, brooms and some bulky sacks.

'I've been having the rubbish thrown out and the place smartened up,' announced Julia as they entered. She seemed pleased to see them and to be able to show off her new authority. 'You're my first clients.' She was leaning over a table writing something carefully on a card, the tip of her tongue sticking out of her mouth and moving slowly sideways as she wrote. The Band Room was otherwise empty.

'You've moved the table tennis table,' said Annabel.

'I didn't move it myself, to be precise,' said Julia. 'I had it moved, which is different. I told you it ought to be in that recess, didn't I?'

'There isn't room to play table tennis there.'

'Don't argue with the Band Room Monitor.'

Annabel's brow darkened but she maintained her resolve. She got the table tennis equipment out of the store-room and, helped by Kate, put the net up. Julia, meanwhile, was sticking her notice on the wall. It was forbidding smoking, gambling and noisy games.

41

'Nobody'll come,' observed Annabel to Kate, serving the ball. 'There'll be nothing for them to do.'

'I heard that,' said Julia, looking round. 'You're making a lot of noise yourselves with that silly table tennis.'

'You have to hit the ball. It's an essential part of the game.'

'Then hit it *quietly*,' crowed Julia. She seemed to like the sound of that for she cackled over it and then came and stood behind Annabel and repeated it. 'Hit it *quietly*.' Annabel groaned.

'There isn't even anybody to hear us,' said Kate, sarcastically.

'*I'm* here,' cried Julia triumphantly. She liked that too and started cackling again, just by Annabel's shoulder.

Annabel slammed her bat down. 'My resolve is weakening, Kate,' she said. 'In fact it's weakened.'

'I didn't have much,' said Kate. 'Anyway, there's no room to play here.'

Julia was giggling as they put the equipment away and left.

'I told you, Kate,' said Annabel, morosely. 'She'll get worse and worse. She's just flexing her muscles.'

A First Year boy was hanging around outside the door. Kate recognized him as the one who'd been sitting alone at a table on the previous day. He had a nervous blink and untidy fair hair which hung over his eyes and which he kept on pushing back with his fingers. His uniform was big enough to last him till the Third Year.

'I was wondering if it was all right to go in there,' he said to them sheepishly.

'I didn't see any notices forbidding it,' Annabel told him, 'but you'd better hurry just in case.' She held the door open for him. Richard White and Damian Price and some Second Years were converging on the place, coming to sniff at the new atmosphere.

'Kate, it's amazing,' said Annabel as they walked away. 'It's exactly like Mavis at St Babs. She started by throwing her weight around in the Games Room. It's like that picture story coming to life. It's uncanny . . .

'It's not just Julia either. The whole school's rotten with injustice. Only at Willers would they make Julia Band Room Monitor in the first place. Willers and St Babs. Other schools aren't as daft, are they, Kate? Kate, tell me other schools aren't as daft.'

Annabel was becoming steadily more agitated.

'Kate, if they're going to behave like St Babs I think we ought to as well. We need a Silent Three to fight injustice too.'

'It wouldn't be so easy in real life as in a comic,' said Kate soothingly. She wasn't taking Annabel seriously.

But Annabel was quickening her pace. 'Let's find a pen and some paper. At least we can give Julia a fright if nothing else. You know how nervous she is.'

The Silent Three was coming to Lord Willoughby's.

Chapter 4

✳✳✳✳✳

Just before the end of dinner break Julia was alone in the Band Room and preparing to leave when a stone with a message tied to it came flying in through the partly open door. The stone bounced off a wall and the message, which had been insecurely attached by string, fell off.

Julia sprang aside, startled, and cowered against the opposite wall. After a few moments, no further stones having arrived, she ventured cautiously over to the piece of paper and picked it up gingerly. Annabel, who had thrown it in, was meanwhile darting to join Kate who was crouched by the window. She arrived there in time to see Julia read the note:

BEWARE, JULIA CHANNING!
YOUR EVIL TYRANNY HAS NOT GONE UNOBSERVED
BEWARE! ERE YOU SUFFER VENGEANCE FROM
THE SILENT THREE!

Julia was seen to start nervously and then, suddenly realizing that she might be watched, to glance quickly round at the window while superimposing a sickly sneer on her face. Annabel and Kate ducked and fled behind those same bamboo clumps into which Julia had thrown the shoes. Annabel had liked the look of that sneer. There had been a twitch to it.

From behind the bamboo clumps they were able to watch as Julia appeared at the Band Room door.

'I can guess who wrote this silly note,' she shouted to the world at large. 'I bet it's somebody whose name rhymes with dunce helped by somebody whose names rhymes with old socks. Well, I've read about the Silent Three in old comics too because we've got some in our house. So HA, HA, HA.'

Julia then ostentatiously locked the Band Room door and swaggered off with much bravado.

Despite the total accuracy of Julia's speech Annabel looked greatly cheered.

'She's nervous, isn't she, Kate,' she said with satisfaction. 'Look how she's walking. As if she's waiting for a bomb to go off behind her.'

'Not looking back,' said Kate, impressed by the effectiveness of Annabel's plan.

'Frightened of what she might see. Three cloaked, hooded figures closing in on her with outstretched talons. She thinks it's us, Kate, but she's not quite sure . . . there's a teeny-weeny little doubt. Maybe the Silent Three have materialized out of one of those dusty old comics . . . oh, Kate, if only we had some robes and masks and could do it properly.'

'We haven't though, have we,' said Kate, not altogether sorry.

Julia's walk was becoming ever more rapid and

Annabel sighed. Giving Julia a fright was pleasing but it was frustrating that there was nothing more they could do.

'I suppose we could complain to Mrs da Susa,' said Kate, as they made their way back towards the school. 'I don't like complaining, though, even about Julia.'

Nor did Annabel. Even about Julia it was unthinkable. It was frustrating again, though, to enter the classroom and see Julia recovered from her fright and casting smug and knowing glances at them while deep in airy and probably boastful conversation with Tracey Cooke. Why was Tracey Cooke listening to her with apparent interest and admiration? Why wasn't she shunning Julia as she ought? Tracey Cooke would make a good candidate for Freda.

Anyway, even if they had been prepared to complain it wouldn't have been any use as they were soon to realize. The ground had already been cut from under their feet.

Both Richard White and Damian Price were looking unusually subdued and at break Annabel and Kate learned why. Apparently Julia had been bossing them around in the Band Room too, banning some game or other and, said Richard White indignantly, they had immediately organized a delegation to protest to Mrs da Susa. They had, however, received no satisfaction whatever, having been peremptorily sent packing.

It was easy to see why, as Annabel commented depressedly to Kate on their way home later. From the names mentioned it was clear that the delegation had been composed of the most shiftless elements of the Second and Third Years with some harmless fodder such as Miles Noggins dragged along to give it an air of desperate respectability. Mrs da Susa would have instantly recognized it for what it was, at attempt by the gambling fraternity to make sure they could continue their activities undisturbed. Nothing could have been better calculated to reinforce Julia's position and convince Mrs da Susa that Julia was doing an excellent job. Any further complaints now would certainly be a waste of time even if they had wanted to make them. It was extremely frustrating.

On Monday, however, matters took a more serious and dramatic turn; in Annabel's view, anyway.

Annabel and Kate were sitting on their favourite bench at dinner break when the First Year boy with the untidy hair they'd last seen entering the Band Room on Friday came and sat down on the other end of it. He was lost in his own thoughts and when Annabel leaned over and poked him on the shoulder he jumped.

'Did you get into the Band Room all right on Friday?' she asked him.

'Er – yes,' he replied, flicking his hair back diffidently.

Kate regarded him with interest. She was wondering why he looked so depressed and also what it was he'd been doing in the Band Room, anyway. Not many First Years went in there alone. Annabel was obviously wondering the same for she leaned over again.

'What did you want to do in the Band Room?' she asked him. 'Wasn't it you I saw sitting at a table last week? Were you playing a game?'

'I was making something,' he said. He seemed inclined to stop there but pinioned by Annabel's penetrating gaze he added, reluctantly, 'I've been carving a chess set.'

'A chess set! A proper one? All the pawns and pieces?'

Annabel was so clearly interested and impressed that he responded. He reached into his pocket. 'That's one of them,' he said, handing it to her. The piece was a knight, the horse's head quite delicately carved.

'That's really good,' said Annabel. 'Better than a lot I've seen in the shops. Are they all as good as that? What do you make them with?'

'I've got a penknife with some attachments on. That and sandpaper.'

'That's really talented.' She handed it to Kate. 'Look, Kate.'

'Where did you learn to do this?' asked Kate, also impressed.

'Picked it up. It's patience mostly. Takes a long time.'

Kate handed it back. 'Must be difficult working in the Band Room with all that racket going on.'

'There's nowhere at home. Anyway, Mum says I get on her nerves sitting around making a mess while she's trying to do things or watch telly.'

Annabel clucked sympathetically. 'You see, Kate,' she said in a private whisper, 'it's amazing. This boy –' she turned back to him for a moment '– what's your name?'

'Charlie Ash.'

She reverted to her whisper. 'Charlie Ash is actually using the Band Room for *the purpose for which it was most intended*. He must be the only one. *He* is what those original ideals were all about.'

She turned back to him again, 'And what are you going to do with the chess set? Do you play chess yourself?'

'Yes. I'm in the Junior Chess Club. But this was going to be a special set. I was going to enter it for the AACA wood-carving competition.'

Annabel and Kate had heard about the competition. AACA – pronounced as 'Arca' – was the Addendon Arts and Crafts Association, formed the previous year. This was their first competition.

'That's for all ages, isn't it,' she said. 'To do well in that would be really something.' And privately, to Kate: 'That would bring some credit to Willers, wouldn't it, Kate, perhaps the first it's ever had.' Then to Charlie Ash again: 'What do you mean, though, *were* going to enter it? Aren't you going to now? Where's the rest of the set?'

He blinked several times very rapidly.

'It's been confiscated.'

'*Confiscated?* Who by?'

'The new Band Room Monitor.'

Annabel rose to her feet slowly and magnificently. It wasn't an ordinary rage, it was a double one, fuelled partly by the confiscation itself and partly by hearing the unspeakable Julia referred to so respectfully by this innocent, unworldly, First Year boy.

'Why?'

'She said I was making a mess.'

'But that's what the place is for. It's another Willers injustice. When's the closing date for entries to this competition?'

'This week. Saturday. I'd just about finished it.'

'We'll get it back for you, won't we, Kate? We won't stand any nonsense from Julia —'

He started blinking nineteen to the dozen. 'Better not. She'd make trouble. She's got it in for me.'

'How could she do that?' asked Kate, who was rather less sure than Annabel about being able to get their way with Julia.

'She says I've been breaking into the Band Room at night. She says she's got positive proof and if I make a fuss about the chess set she'll go straight to Mrs da Susa and tell her.'

Kate was perplexed. 'But have you been breaking into the Band Room or haven't you?'

'No. Honest. But she's so certain I have and she's so well in with Mrs da Susa that it doesn't make any difference.'

'Then what's this proof she's talking about?'

'She says there's a mess left when she comes in, in the morning.'

Annabel's face had become still darker. 'She must have made it up to frighten you. It's exactly what Julia would do.'

'You oughtn't to let it worry you,' Kate advised

him, but he didn't look convinced. He shut both eyes tightly in an enormous blink, contorting his face to do so.

Annabel had heard enough. 'You don't have to bother about anything any more,' she told him, magnificently. 'We'll get your chess set back for you without getting you into trouble, won't we, Kate. We'll do it subtly.'

He looked up at her, as did Kate. He was two years younger than Annabel and in some ways younger than his years. To him she probably looked quite important. Kate watched him brighten.

'Will you? Honestly?'

'Leave it to us. It's time we went, Kate.'

'*Thanks.*' Kate found the gratitude unnerving, especially as it was partly directed at her. As she rose too he hesitated and then said: 'I think she's got it in for me for another reason. She came to the Chess Club on Saturday. There was her and me and Julian Parlane –'

'Did you beat her?' asked Annabel, eagerly.

'She couldn't get the hang of it. She knocked the board over.'

That restored Annabel's good humour, but only briefly. She was too overwhelmed by the rest of what she'd heard. As soon as they were out of earshot she exploded.

'Kate, it's getting more and more uncanny. First we've got Julia being a tyrant. Now there's a Great Injustice.'

'I know, Annabel, I know.' Kate was recalling the look of gratitude on Charlie Ash's face. And also the many impulsive promises made in the past by Annabel. 'But what can we do?'

'Kate, we *must* have a Silent Three to put the wind up Julia and make her back down. Do you realize, Kate, that Charlie Ash probably really *is* gifted. Oh, where can we get some robes and masks?'

'I shouldn't think we can, Annabel.'

Cowardly it may have been, but the 'thank goodness' was unspoken.

*

'What sort of robes do you mean, exactly?' inquired Sheena Franks-Walters. 'We've got some long, grey ones with hoods. They're the sort monks used to wear, but I suppose that's not what you're looking for.'

She ran her finger round the inside of the carton from which she had been eating something rather delicious-looking and licked it, eyes bulging slightly. Annabel, who had been walking away, froze in her tracks.

It was afternoon break and Annabel and Kate had paused in the dining-hall to mention to Sheena that they couldn't at that moment carry on with table tennis tuition because of the situation at the Band Room. Sheena had taken the news philosophically and as they had started to continue their progress towards the door Annabel had added, darkly, simply out of frustration, 'I just wish we had some masks and robes, that's all.' Sheena had then made her comment.

'Masks aren't a problem. We've plenty of those.' She put the carton down and patted her lips with a handkerchief.

Annabel retraced her steps. 'Grey masks?'

'Yes, I think so,' said Sheena, screwing up her eyes in an effort to remember. 'Yes, I see what you mean. It would be a pity not to have them matching, wouldn't it. I'm sure they are. I used to see them when I was looking for dressing-up clothes in Mummy's theatrical boxes.'

'It's fate,' breathed Annabel.

Kate wasn't quite as grateful for the news. 'Was your mother an actress, then?'

'Not a proper actress. I don't think Mummy's ever done any proper work. But she used to organize amateur things.'

'But that's marvellous,' Annabel was thrilled. 'Can you lend us some, Sheena? Say, two –' she glanced at Kate – 'no, three robes and three masks!'

'I expect so,' said Sheena. 'What do you want them for? A play?'

Annabel hesitated. To Kate, her thoughts were transparent. To be a Silent Three they needed three. Clearly she, Kate, was cast as one of them. They could hardly borrow the equipment from Sheena without at least offering her the choice of being the third. Apart from the ingratitude it would have obvious dangers. True, Sheena would hardly be one's first choice as a daring companion in a secret organization but . . .

Annabel glanced at Kate but Kate wasn't giving any help.

'Sheena,' she said tentatively, 'how would you like to be a fighter against tyranny at Willers, a champion of justice?'

Sheena considered it. 'Whose tyranny?'

Annabel's face darkened. 'Who else's but –' she began, then paused. 'Just a sec,' she said, 'I don't think I can tell you that yet.' She drew Kate aside.

'Kate, it's fate,' she whispered. 'We can't miss a chance like this. I think we should ask Sheena if she'd like to be the third member of the Silent Three but we've got to rub it into her that it's a secret. We've got to make it seem important – do things properly – have a meeting-place where we can initiate her and that sort of thing. Got any ideas?'

'You haven't said yet who's going to be the second member,' Kate whispered back rebelliously, then regretted the remark. 'Only a joke, Annabel.'

'They used to meet in the crypt,' mused Annabel. 'Willers doesn't have a crypt but there's the boiler room . . . that's underground and nobody goes there except Mr Rumator.'

Mr Rumator was the groundsman, a friend of Annabel's.

'That would mean coming back to Willers out of school hours.'

'But there's nowhere else, is there, Kate?' Annabel turned back to Sheena.

'Sheena, if you *would* like to fight tyranny, then I – er – I suggest you go to the boiler room at – er – seven o'clock this evening. Is that possible?'

Sheena looked puzzled. She hadn't read any old comics. 'What for?'

'You'll find out when you get there,' Annabel replied patiently. Then, as Sheena continued to look puzzled: 'I don't want to anticipate anything but it's possible you *might* be asked to join some sort of secret organization and that the robes and masks you mentioned might be useful so bring – take those with you. Three of each. Three robes. Three masks.'

'You mean you're going to be there,' gurgled Sheena, knowingly. 'That does sound fun.'

Annabel sighed. 'But can you be there? Tonight? It's urgent.'

A slow smile dawned upon Sheena's plumply pretty face. 'I'd love to,' she said with sudden unusual eagerness. 'It's just what I need to fill in the time.'

'Fill in what time?'

Sheena dropped her voice a little. 'It's my Youth Club night. Daddy's insisted I join the Youth Club. He says I ought to mix with the young people of Addendon. Bennion's driving me there every Tuesday and Thursday.'

Annabel and Kate heard this with interest. It certainly sounded in keeping with the egalitarian views of the phenomenally wealthy Mr Franks-Walters. It wasn't enough, apparently, to send Sheena to Lord Willoughby's to mix with the masses, the salt of the earth, there. She had to have the full treatment.

'What do you do when you get there?' asked Annabel.

'I hide round the back of the hall. I did go in the

first time and tried to play table tennis but I wasn't any good and they were all beastly.to me.'

'The young people of Addendon were?'

'They're rather rough; even rougher than some of the boys at Lord Willoughby's. Some of them are older and bigger.'

'Have you told your father this?'

'Daddy thinks I ought to persevere. He's convinced they're very good-hearted beneath their rough exteriors and I expect he's right because Daddy always is. That's why I'm trying to learn table tennis properly because it might change their attitude towards me. I'm also,' continued Sheena, 'troyin' ter learn ter speak inner common accent. It's moy Dad's oidea. 'E sez I talk too lah-di-dah.'

This last was a demonstration of Sheena's common accent and having delivered it she lowered her eyes and blushed.

'But, anyway,' she added, reverting to her normal bray, 'that's lovely for tonight. Instead of hanging about behind the Youth Centre I shall be able to come to the boiler room instead. It sounds warmer.'

'Don't forget the robes and masks,' warned Annabel, 'and that it's a secret.'

Sheena tittered. 'I shall guard it with my life,' she said, insincerely.

'It's a pity it had to be Sheena who's got the robes and masks,' said Annabel later, on the way home. 'She's a bit of a weak link. Still, beggars can't be choosers and all that really matters is that we *are* going to have a Silent Three. I can't wait to get back to school and put our robes on and initiate Sheena, can you, Kate? Then look out, Julia Channing! We'll stop your little games!

'I think, Kate, that once we've got a Silent Three we ought to keep it in existence always, ready at a moment's notice to don its robes when needed and go forth to fight injustices and keep Willers on the rails. It's exciting, isn't it. Are you excited, Kate?'

Kate was dazed. She was feeling like a character in a comic.

Chapter 5

✶✶✶✶✶

'Who's there?' demanded the shadowy figure in the dark recesses of the boiler room that evening.

'It's me,' tittered Sheena, who had just stumbled in down the steps. 'Is that you, Annabel?'

'Have you brought what you were asked to bring?' said the shadowy figure, coldly.

'The robes and masks? Yes.'

'Then throw them over.'

'All of them? What about my own?'

'All of them. You are not yet a member of the Silent Three. You have not been initiated.'

'Here you are, then.'

There was a little grunt of satisfaction and excitement as the shadowy figure caught the robes and masks and proceeded to examine them briefly before passing on one set to a second shadowy figure beside her, who took it gingerly. There was some whispering – 'try them on,' the first shadowy figure was saying – then a good deal of heaving and pulling and snapping of mask elastic while Sheena waited patiently. This was followed by murmurs of delight from the first shadowy figure.

'Bit long, aren't they?' murmured the second shadowy figure who seemed less sure about the whole thing.

'I'll hem them up on Mum's machine some time,' replied the first.

'When can I put mine on?' asked Sheena, impatient to join the fun.

'Hang on a minute,' said the first shadowy figure. 'Do you mind if we paint numbers on the hoods?'

Since Sheena did not, a small bottle of whitening with a little brush in the cap was produced. There was some modest demurring by the first shadowy figure about having the 'l' on her hood but the second was insistent, saying that she was the leader and welcome to it. The second shadowy figure then had a '2' painted on her hood and a '3' was painted on the remaining one.

The first shadowy figure, now to be known as Number One, then invited Sheena to take a seat on an upturned box while the two robed, hooded and masked figures sat down on other upturned boxes facing her. A fourth upturned box, performing the role of table and covered by a cut-up old black skirt, was between them and on this stood a spluttering candle in a saucer, the only source of light in the room.

When they were all settled, Number One began. Her voice was stern.

'Sheena Franks-Walters, it is time for your initiation. Have you, Sheena Franks-Walters, come here determined to fight against tyranny and injustice at Lord Willoughby's School?'

'I really came here to fill in the time when I'm supposed to be at the Youth Club,' tittered Sheena, who was by now quivering with excitement, 'but I'd love to fight tyranny and injustice, too. I'm sure that's very important.'

'Please don't be silly and frivolous,' commanded Number One. 'This is a very serious matter. And please address me as Number One.'

'I'm sorry, Number One,' squeaked Sheena, contrite. 'It's only because I'm so excited.'

'Sheena Franks-Walters, if you are allowed to join us do you swear at all times to work for our cause and never to betray our secrets? Answer with your right hand raised.'

'I do.'

'Then I can tell you that the name of the evil tyrant is Julia Channing. She has among other things wronged a First Year, Charlie Ash. Do you, Sheena Franks-Walters, vow not to rest until the wrong is righted and her tyranny brought to an end?'

'I do.'

'Then I name you a worthy member of the Silent Three. Rise and step forward, you who were Sheena Franks-Walters, to receive your robe and mask and become – Number Three.'

Sheena rose obediently to be helped into robes and hood. The figure 3, painted over-hastily, proved to be upside-down. Also, there was something funny about the mask.

'This one's got a funny nose on,' said Number Two, turning it over in her hands.

'I must have brought a comic one by mistake,' tutted Sheena.

'Then tear it off and replace the mask as soon as you can,' said Number One, sharply. The mask elastic snapped unnecessarily hard against the back of Sheena's head as Number One put it on for her.

'And now what?' asked Number Two as they sat down.

'The first step,' said Number One, 'is to show the tyrant that we really exist by letting her see us in our robes. That on its own might give her a big enough fright to bring her to heel. I think we should soften her up with another warning message at dinner break tomorrow, delivered in our robes, then hit her hard in some way in the evening.'

'I couldn't come tomorrow evening, Number One,' said Number Three apologetically. 'Daddy's only letting me have the car when I go to the Youth Club and that's not till the day after.'

'Well, Thursday, then,' said Number One. 'I suppose we can wait till then.'

'Where would we deliver this note?' inquired Number Two.

'At the Band Room, of course.'

Number Three started tittering nervously again. 'We might be seen by other people.'

'Hope so.'

There was silence.

'I take it,' said Number One, 'that silence means you agree. In which case' – she turned away and, hoisting up her robe, rummaged discreetly underneath it to produce a Biro and pad of paper from her blazer pockets – 'I will draft a message.'

Thus was composed the message which appears at the beginning of this narrative.

Then, business being concluded, this first

meeting of the Silent Three was declared closed. Sheena removed her robe and left instantly, being anxious not to keep Bennion waiting. (Not so much, apparently, because she really minded his discovering that she hadn't been to the Youth Club – Bennion being capable of considerable discretion – but more from a feeling that being parked outside the Addendon Youth Centre at turning-out time was no place for the sensitive chauffeur of an expensive limousine.)

Annabel and Kate then stacked the boxes, stuffed the Silent Three wardrobes and the table cover to the very back of the topmost of some disused and cobwebby shelves, extinguished the candle and put that there too, then departed also, stumbling up the steps in the darkness.

'It's been an historic evening, Kate,' Annabel commented with much satisfaction as they closed the door behind them. But, as they were quickly to discover, it wasn't over yet.

The light was fading as they made their way from the boiler room, which is at the rear of the main building at Lord Willoughby's, to the school gates. This route took them past the new gardens and shrubberies which Annabel's friend Mr Rumator had been working to create over the past few years, ever since the school had grown in size and its grounds extended. Annabel was very fond of these gardens and always ready to remind people that, in her view, Mr Rumator was the one person at Lord Willoughby's doing anything useful and constructive around the place.

Suddenly, Annabel halted, listening.

'There's somebody behind those bushes, Kate,' she whispered.

Kate could hear the sounds of movement, too; scraping noises mostly. An animal, perhaps . . . ?

'It sounds like someone *digging*,' she whispered back.

Annabel hurried a little way further along the drive on tiptoe and then, crouching stealthily, turned in among the shrubs. Kate followed and was in time to see Annabel, now little more than a silhouette, go down on one knee in order to peer between some branches. Kate dropped down beside her.

They were looking into a sort of clearing, created by the art of Mr Rumator. To one side of the clearing a gnarled, spreading old holm oak, the tree around which Mr Rumator had originally created his scheme, threw out a huge branch parallel with the ground. It was a branch well known to Annabel and Kate. When in the First Year, they had played on it during many a dinner break. It was a wonderful branch for walking along, for somersaulting over and hanging backwards from by the knees. They had given up that sort of thing now but every First Year homed in on it.

The ground beneath the branch had been dug over recently, presumably by Mr Rumator with the intention of further planting. Digging there now, turning over the earth with a fork and examining it closely as she did so, was a girl.

It was Julia Channing!

The sight was so amazing that Kate started to gasp the name but thought better of it. Julia must have heard the slight sound, however, for she paused in her digging to look nervously about her. Then, apparently becoming fearful as she surveyed the gathering darkness she suddenly turned and fled, carrying her fork with her.

'Well!' said Annabel. They rose and went over to the spot where Julia had been digging. Annabel kicked at the earth with her toe but there was nothing to be seen.

'She seemed to be looking for something,' said Kate.

'A hoard of stolen jewels, perhaps?' suggested Annabel. There was not in her voice as much irony as Kate would have expected; more relish.

Extraordinary though that was, there was yet more to come. As they returned to the drive, discussing what they'd seen, Kate happened to glance across the playing fields.

'There's a light on in the Band Room,' she said and halted again to stare. Annabel followed suit.

It couldn't be Julia. She wouldn't have had time to get there even if she had run in that direction, which she hadn't. Who then? The Band Room was supposed to be closed and locked up for the evening.

As they watched, the light blinked out, the door opened and someone emerged. At this distance and in that light the figure was unrecognizable. The only certainties were that it was a man and that he was wearing some cherry-red garment, a sweater perhaps or a jacket. It didn't look like any of the masters and anyway there was no reason for a master to be there in the evening.

The man paused for a moment, apparently locking the door, then went out of sight behind the Band Room, making for the Apsley Road exit from the school grounds. Kate was left with an impression of someone rather small and jaunty. Willers masters weren't jaunty.

'Come on, Kate,' cried Annabel, gathering herself. She shot off across the playing fields in pursuit and Kate followed. Passing the Band Room they ran down the path to Apsley Road but there was no one to be seen. Apsley Road was merely deserted pools of lamplight. Perhaps he'd had transport or he might simply have walked quickly. They went back to the Band Room and tried the door. It was locked.

Annabel was breathing hard and it wasn't only exertion. Her eye was bright. 'Kate, who do you think that was?'

'I can't imagine, Annabel. Somebody with a key by the look of it.'

'So Julia was right. Somebody *is* getting into the Band Room at night but it's not Charlie Ash. But who? Why?'

'Kate, it's amazing . . . Julia digging secretly in the grounds at night . . . a mystery intruder in the Band Room. We haven't only got a Tyranny and a Great Injustice at Willers now. We've got a Mystery Man and a Deep Game as well!'

★

They walked home in the lamplight, animatedly discussing these extraordinary developments.

Should they tell anyone? Annabel thought not. This was so clearly a job for the Silent Three.

Was there a connection between Julia's digging and the Mystery Man? Annabel's view was that it was highly likely.

Had Julia really believed it was Charlie Ash when she had accused him of breaking into the Band Room? In Annabel's opinion anyone digging furtively as Julia had been was up to something pretty nefarious and not to be trusted, even if Julia were to be trusted under normal circumstances which she wasn't. It was quite possible that she was trying to pin the blame on Charlie in order to protect an accomplice, presumably upon orders since Julia was incapable of making a decision herself.

One thing was certain, Annabel decided, taking from her pocket the note she had composed in the boiler room and screwing it up: *that* was out of date.

'We're going to need a new note, Kate. We'll deliver it at dinner break tomorrow, then after school's over I suggest we come back in the light and see if we can spot that mystery man again, and try to find what it is that Julia's looking for. Is that agreed, Number Two?'

'There's no point, I suppose,' Kate suggested tentatively, 'in just asking Julia at school tomorrow?'

'Oh, Kate,' said Annabel and she sighed tolerantly.

Kate had to admit to herself that it was all

extremely odd. More and yet more she had the feeling of living in a comic.

'Agreed, Number One.'

Chapter 6

*****

During dinner break on the following day Mrs da Susa decided to visit the Band Room to see how Julia was progressing. This wasn't because of any doubts about the decision to make her Band Room Monitor. On the contrary, she was hoping to gloat a little over its success, believing the complaints she had received to be evidence of the zeal and enthusiasm with which Julia was approaching her new responsibilities.

She was passing the playing fields when she was startled to see two grey-robed, hooded and masked figures emerge from the shelter of some trees and run towards the Band Room. 'Good heavens!' she exclaimed and halted.

Unaware of being observed, the leader of the two hooded figures glanced back over his or her shoulder and then paused. Seeing this, the second one did likewise. They were evidently waiting for someone, and a moment later a third hooded figure came hopping and staggering out of the trees with its foot caught in the hem of its robe. The leading figure beckoned with evident irritation and then, losing patience, ran on again. Stopping beside the Band Room it made to hurl something through the open window.

Just as the object was leaving its hand, the first

hooded figure was startled by a cry from the second which pointed at Mrs da Susa. It was difficult to be sure but Mrs da Susa thought it was a girl's voice calling something like 'Number One'. The throw went wildly astray and the object, instead of going through the window, hit the wall and fell to the ground. Both hooded figures then fled, pausing only to help the third, which had fallen over, to its feet and bundle it back amongst the trees.

Mrs da Susa, who had stood staring as if mesmerized, collected herself and went to investigate the object which the leading figure had tried to throw into the Band Room. It proved to be a stone with a message taped to it. The message read:

JULIA CHANNING BEWARE!
WE KNOW OF THE GREAT INJUSTICE
YOU HAVE COMMITTED AND THE DEEP GAME
YOU ARE PLAYING.
YOU WILL HEAR FROM US AGAIN SOON!
(sgd) THE SILENT THREE

Mrs da Susa stared at it, then mechanically removed it from the stone, folded it neatly and put it in her pocket, detaching the tape which she also put in her pocket to be tidily disposed of later. She then returned to the school having decided to postpone her visit to the Band Room while she reflected. She was considerably shaken by what she had seen, coming so soon after reading the comics.

The postponement was really rather fortunate for Julia, who was seated alone in the Band Room doing nothing but noisily crushing a large mint between her teeth and gazing reflectively into space. The discovery that everyone had stopped coming might have given Mrs da Susa pause in her self-congratulation.

Julia, wrapped in her own thoughts, had heard nothing of the events outside. She had been subdued all morning as Annabel and Kate had observed with satisfaction and interest.

In the boiler room, meanwhile, the Silent Three disrobed and bickered, Sheena maintaining that it wasn't her fault that she'd kept on tripping over her robe: it was too long and Annabel hadn't kept her promise to hem it up: anyway, they wouldn't have been able to have a Silent Three if it weren't for her; and, moreover, Annabel and Kate ought to have seen Mrs da Susa before she saw them.

Annabel conceded that she'd panicked and mis-directed the stone with the message on it and that it was now presumably in Mrs da Susa's hands. However, she wasn't sorry that it had happened. She didn't agree with Kate, who was worried about being seen by Mrs da Susa. Why shouldn't Mrs da Susa be aware of the Silent Three and the unrest within the school? It was a good thing! To be a proper Silent Three they needed to be talked about.

Kate wasn't so sure about that. Surely there was something wrong there?

Sheena unexpectedly eased the tension with a little joke. 'Yes, it's good for Mrs da Susa to *get the message*,' she said suddenly, and laughed a plump laugh with a little snort in it. Her little joke made her forget the little rage she'd been in and she kept on laughing at intervals while they put the robes away.

Anyway, as Annabel said to Kate later, that had been mere window dressing, a flexing of the Silent Three's muscles, a preliminary to the real business which would begin that evening, luckily without Number Three being there to get in the way.

Annabel was feverishly impatient to discover the object of Julia's search. She had lain awake on the previous night thinking about it and had speculated about it to Kate during lessons. She always came to one of two conclusions. It was either a small oilskin bag from which, when opened, would pour a glittering cascade of priceless gems or else it was a small iron-bound chest which, when the rusty lock had been turned and the lid prised open, would prove to contain a similar glittering array of priceless gems.

That evening, they found out what it really was. Or, at any rate, what they assumed it must be.

They discovered it quite quickly, only minutes after they had arrived stealthily with their garden forks borrowed from home and, having made sure that Julia wasn't around, started turning over the ground where she had been digging.

It was Annabel who brought it to the surface. It wasn't what she had been anticipating but she found it almost as thrilling.

It was a key; a large, old-fashioned, ornate key.

Although they watched the Band Room for a while, no one came that night. And Julia didn't return. But for the moment the key was enough. More than enough!

Mrs da Susa brought the existence of the Silent Three to the school's attention next morning while taking Assembly in the absence of Mr Trimm. She left the announcement till last.

'Yesterday,' she began, sternly, 'whilst on my way to the Junior Leisure and Recreation Centre I saw three robed, hooded and masked figures running across the school grounds.'

She paused. She had the sensation of hearing her own voice from a distance and what she had just said sounded absurd. But she was only recounting the literal truth, was she not?

'From a note which fell into my possession I gather that this – er – this organization calls itself the Silent Three and appears to believe that it is fighting injustice and what it calls "a deep game".'

Again she paused, frowning, then realized why those words felt familiar, as if they had been used before.

They *had* been used before; by Miss Sterndale, Headmistress of St Babs. She, Mrs da Susa, had been repeating a speech balloon from a picture story in an old comic.

The feeling of living out the role of a character in an old comic was heightened as her eye caught that of Julia Channing. Julia was sitting bolt upright and staring at her with a fixed, anxious expression. The resemblance to Mavis was remarkable.

Mrs da Susa removed her gaze to the ceiling and ploughed on.

'I will overlook the incident on this occasion but I would advise anyone with information about injustices or "deep games" to bring it to me and not to try to settle grievances in their own way.'

She collected her papers and left the platform hurriedly because it had been dawning upon her while speaking that she had been borrowing from St Babs again. Those identical words had been Miss Sterndale's next speech balloon. She had been unable to get away from her.

Out in the corridor she turned towards her study then checked herself. What had Miss Sterndale done at this juncture? Yes, she had gone to *her* study, there to sit down and indulge in a "thinks" balloon about the Silent Three.

Resolutely, Mrs da Susa turned and went off in the opposite direction. She would *not* be a Miss Sterndale. She would break away from her *now*.

The guessing and probing as to the identity of the Silent Three started while everyone was still filing out of Assembly.

'Bet Annabel Bunce and Kate Stocks are two of 'em,' said Richard White. He was standing with Damian Price just outside the door.

Annabel shrugged one shoulder. 'That could be bluff,' she said, 'to throw suspicion off you two.'

'Gurn. Boys wouldn't go round calling themselves the Silent Three. Would they, Dame?'

'Intelligent boys would,' said Annabel coldly.

Damian Price took an independent line. 'I dunno. There's a lot of injustices at Willers. Something needs doing about it.'

They went off. Miles Noggins had been listening. 'I think something like that's needed at Willers,' he agreed. 'I wouldn't mind joining an organization like the Silent Three.'

Annabel eyed him speculatively as he propelled his stout frame onwards in the direction of French.

'Was he hinting at something?' inquired Kate, thinking that he was welcome to her place if he really wanted it.

'He could be useful,' said Annabel. 'Why're people assuming it's something to do with us, though?'

They were joined by Sheena. She spoke in a slightly suppressed shriek. 'I say, isn't it thrilling. I almost burst when Mrs da Susa talked about us in Assembly. I was so proud. I wanted to stand up and tell everyone I'm a member. I had to restrain myself.'

'Keep your voice down,' said Annabel tersely. 'Julia's just behind us. And go on. We oughtn't to be seen together.' Sheena padded off, piqued.

Julia strode past them trying to look haughty but without succeeding, restoring Annabel's spirits.

'She looks anxious, doesn't she, Kate. Frightened, too. The Silent Three's already had an effect.'

Kate had to admit to herself that that was so, though why the Silent Three should, on its record so far, have frightened anybody, even Julia, she couldn't imagine. Indeed, if she were to disassociate herself from Annabel's enthusiasm, which wasn't easy to do, she had to ask herself whether it was likely that Julia was involved in any deep games.

But there *was* an injustice. There *was* a 'mystery man'. Julia *had* been digging secretly in the grounds at night apparently looking for a key. You couldn't get around those facts.

Annabel herself didn't have any doubts. The plan of action was ready. They had found the key but now they needed to know what it meant to Julia. What lock did it fit? Did it have any direct connection with the Mystery Man or Charlie Ash's chess set?

And they needed that chess set back. Urgently.

Shock tactics, Annabel believed, were the answer.

'Tonight, Kate, we haunt her. We flit about and appear at the window of her study –'

'She hasn't got a study. This is Willers, not St Babs.'

' – I mean her den at home. Then at the right moment when she's scared out of her wits we confront her with the key and what we know and she'll break down and confess what she's up to. She's bound to. Whatever's going on, Julia will be the weak link in it, the part that cracks first –'

'Better get into French. We're last.'

' – and speaking of weak links, I'm fed up with Sheena. She'd be bound to ruin everything. All that tripping and giggling and I'm sure she hasn't even got the hang of what the Great Injustice is all about.'

'To be fair, have we told her?'

'She hasn't asked.'

'But we can't just drop her. They're her robes.'

'Just for this one big evening. It's so important. We could be the Silent Two or the Silent Three with one absent sick.' Annabel mulled it over. 'Or we could give Miles a chance. Sheena's so scatty she won't even remember what we said about tonight.

She'll hang around the back of the Youth Club again.'

'I hope you're right, Annabel.'

Annabel had already put that decision behind her.

'Tonight, Kate, we'll know the answers to everything.'

★

Julia didn't hear the first shower of gravel that rattled against the window of her den at home that evening. She was too absorbed in a video film, a 'creepy'. She was watching it seated on the edge of her chair and it was helping her to forget her homework and certain other matters.

The second shower was thrown with more force and was composed of larger stones and hit the window with a bang just as the Egyptian mummy was rising from its tomb immediately behind the unsuspecting heroine. Julia leapt out of her chair and cowered against the wall.

Outside, crouched in the darkness, Number One spoke irritably. 'For goodness' sake be careful, Number Three. You nearly broke the window.'

'I expect everybody in the house heard *that*,' murmured Number Two.

She was proved at least partially correct by the switching on of a light and the opening not of Julia's window, but of the one above it, upstairs.

'Who's throwing stones out there?' demanded Mrs Channing.

The Silent Three huddled together behind the

inadequate screen of a half-grown buddleia. The Channings' garden lacked mature shrubs.

Unable to see anything, Mrs Channing closed the window and withdrew, grumbling to herself, assuming that the stones had been thrown by a passer-by who had now gone. Meanwhile a large car which had been moving slowly and almost silently along the street stopped two or three doors away and a cloaked and hooded figure got out and proceeded to trot past the houses looking at the numbers. The first the Silent Three knew of its presence was when they heard the voice behind them.

'Honestly!' it said, peevishly. 'You are a couple of old scatters. You didn't tell me you were coming straight here. I've been waiting at the boiler room for you. Bennion had to look up Julia's address in the phone book.'

The Silent Three turned their heads. Sheena was standing on the pavement, spectacularly silhouetted against the lamplight and looking into the Channings' open plan front garden.

'And where's my outfit gone? It's just jolly good luck I brought a shorter robe with me and a new mask.'

Annabel flapped her hand furiously to tell her to get down but Sheena's eyes were becoming accustomed to the gloom. 'There are three of you,' she cried indignantly.

'We're supposed to be the *Silent* Three,' hissed Annabel.

'Four,' Kate corrected her, rolling her eyes in despair.

'Who's the fat one?' shrieked Sheena. Advancing upon Miles she yanked at his hood and he fought her off. The upstairs window opened again.

'Who's making that noise down there?' shouted Mrs Channing. At the same time the curtain of Julia's den was hauled back and her window opened too. The struggling hooded figures, now joined by Annabel trying to separate them, were caught in the stream of light.

'It's the Noisy Three,' jeered Julia, who had recovered from her shock and seemed positively cheered by the sight. 'Annabel Bunce and her noisy friends falling out and fighting among themselves.'

There was a ripping sound. 'Now you've torn Mummy's robe,' hissed Sheena. '*Me* torn it?' grunted Miles.

'I think we ought to dial 999,' shouted Julia. 'I think it's a great injustice the way ordinary decent people like ourselves are prevented from having a quiet evening watching our videos by noisy gangs in robes and masks. I wouldn't be surprised if they didn't come here to break in and steal. They may even be armed. Watch them, Mum, while I ask Daddy to ring the police.'

The word 'police' caught Sheena's attention and she released her hold on Miles's robe. Her voice was suddenly a squeak.

'I mustn't be caught by the police. Daddy would be livid. He thinks I'm at the Youth Club.'

'You should have thought of that before,' hissed the enraged Annabel. 'You're the one who's made a mess of everything.'

Sheena was uninterested. With the nearest thing to a burst of speed that had ever been seen from her, she hoisted up her robe and fled. The panic was catching and she was followed immediately by Miles. Julia meanwhile hung out of her window giggling and jeering. Kate, still crouched behind the buddleia with Annabel, could see her face clearly.

The plan had gone disastrously wrong but so happy did Julia look, so pleased with herself, that Kate was momentarily certain that it didn't matter anyway because they'd got everything so utterly wrong in the first place. Julia had nothing to hide. There was some totally innocent explanation, hard though it was to see what it could be, for why she had been digging in the school grounds.

Then Annabel rose majestically to her feet. She raised the key high above her head. The dramatic build-up had failed but nevertheless she was going to play her trump card for there might never be another opportunity. And Charlie Ash's need of his chess set was urgent.

'Look, Julia Channing,' she cried. 'THE KEY. WE HAVE YOUR GUILTY SECRET!'

The effect was dramatic. Julia's giggle expired abruptly. Her hands gripped the window ledge. Her face sagged. Kate's doubts were immediately dispelled. Julia *did* have a guilty secret.

It was the moment to strike home their advantage and extort a confession from Julia's trembling lips but Annabel didn't get the chance. The Channings' front door opened and someone came storming out.

Numbers One and Two fled.

Chapter 7

*****

They fled not, of course, from any fear of the police – that being merely a taunt on Julia's part – but to avoid being cornered by Julia's father or, worse, her mother. The only comfort was, thought Kate as she leapt over the flower border, that the key appeared to be an issue sensitive enough probably to cause Julia to restrain her mother from reporting all this to Mr Trimm.

Dashing into the street they saw that Sheena was scrambling into the rear seat of the Franks-Walters' limousine, having apparently stopped bothering to keep up any pretence with Bennion and enlisted his co-operation instead. Miles, not caring whether he was wanted or not, was pushing in after her.

'Hold the door, Number Threes,' screeched Annabel and they, too, piled in. Then Bennion, with the air of someone used to far more dramatic happenings than this during his years of service with the Franks-Walters, drove immaculately away with them all in a heap on the rear seat.

In this position they were unaware of Julia racing out of her front door, of her charging down the garden path waving frantically and then running down the street after them in hopeless pursuit, only giving up when they disappeared round the corner at the end of the road. She sat down on a low wall to recover, gasping and choking for breath.

By the time they turned into the High Street they had sorted themselves out, Kate next to the nearside window and Annabel between her and Sheena. Uncharacteristically, Annabel sat slumped in disconsolate silence contemplating the almost total failure of their mission. True, they had confirmed that the key meant a great deal to Julia but Annabel hadn't had any doubts about that anyway. They'd learnt nothing else and they hadn't got Charlie Ash's chess set back. It had been disastrous.

It was at this point that a horn started blaring ferociously and continuously behind them and a long, low racing shape swooped past intent upon forcing them into the side of the road.

Kate's immediate assumption was that it was plain-clothes police and she instinctively ducked, as did the others, before realizing there wasn't any point. They all raised their heads again. The other car, meanwhile, hauled itself to a stop in front of them on screaming brakes.

Bennion brought the limousine quietly to rest. Kate heard the slam of the other car's door and approaching footsteps. At the press of a button by Bennion a window opened and a head stuck itself in.

It was Mr Franks-Walters, Sheena's preposterously wealthy father.

'Saw the car in front,' he said. 'Thought "hallo, that's mine. Must say how-do."'

He was wearing a very ancient yellow and brown checked flat cap and a loud, two-toned yellow checked muffler, knotted at the throat and thrust into the V-neck of his sagging old green sweater. His motoring outfit, presumably. His pipe stuck out of the corner of his mouth. He looked like Toad of Toad Hall.

'Which one of you's Sheena?' he asked heartily, eyeing the row of masked figures on the rear seat. 'I suppose one of you's Sheena.'

'I'm Sheena,' said a small, miserable voice.

'So this is what you do at the Youth Club, is it,' said Mr Franks-Walters indulgently. 'Always wondered what went on there. Vaguely imagined it might be snooker and table tennis but this looks much more fun. Look after 'em, Bennion. Help 'em have a good time. Nice to see the old jalopy's coming in useful. I always believe in sharing what little one has.'

He removed his head and Bennion closed the window. After a few moments they heard him whoomph off again, breaking the speed limit in 3.5 seconds flat. The High Street was silent again save for four palpitating hearts.

After a time Bennion, who had treated the intervention as if it were nothing to do with him, for which Sheena was presumably duly grateful, turned his head. 'Are there any instructions, ma'am?' he inquired.

Annabel leaned forward. She had been taking the opportunity to do some thinking. It might be worthwhile to make one more effort, however despairing, to salvage something from the wreckage of their plans before they all had to go home to bed. 'Mr

Bennion,' she said, 'I wonder if you'd mind driving us to Lord Willoughby's, Apsley Road entrance.'

'Bennion wasn't talking to you,' said Sheena, reviving. 'You can't give him orders. It's not your car.'

'Your dad's just said he wants us to share it,' said Annabel coldly. 'And he wants Bennion to help us have a good time. Anyway,' she added, even more coldly, 'if you want to belong to the Silent Three so badly that you start fighting over it then you've got to obey Number One and expect to have your car commandeered.'

Sheena thought about it. 'Lord Willoughby's, Bennion. Apsley Road entrance.'

'What do you want to go to Willers for?' asked Miles Noggins, lounging back luxuriously and easing his mask. He had had several severe frights that evening but the discovery that membership of the Silent Three brought bonuses such as riding in a car like this was helping him to recover from them. He intended to enjoy it.

'Tell you later,' said Annabel, shortly. Subordinates who fled without waiting for orders in the heat of battle didn't deserve to be kept informed.

To get to Lord Willoughby's they had to re-pass the end of Julia's road. Julia was just rising from the low wall where she had been recovering for some minutes when she saw the car sail by again and instantly made to resume the chase, only to realize that she had a stitch and that in any case direct pursuit was hopeless. But the car's direction, coupled with the fact that it had obviously turned back and was heading purposefully for somewhere after a change of mind, gave her a fairly sure idea of its destination. She hobbled after it, holding her side.

Annabel, meanwhile, was informing Kate of her plans in a whisper. 'I thought we ought to have a look at the Band Room, Kate. It's the only thing we *can* do now this evening. The key's at the centre of this mystery and so is the Band Room. There must be a link between them. And then there's the Mystery Man. He might be there again.'

'It's possible, Annabel.'

The car turned left into Apsley Road where it ran alongside the school grounds and Bennion started to slow in preparation for the entrance. Apsley Road itself was deserted save for a pedestrian striding along the shadowy pavement towards them.

Annabel still sounded depressed. 'It's all we *can* do now, Kate – *down, everybody! Keep going, please, Mr Bennion.*'

Saying which, Annabel pushed Sheena to the floor and fell on top of her. Kate and Miles slid down obediently.

'What do you think you're doing?' Sheena demanded indignantly in a muffled voice.

'That was Mrs da Susa.'

Sheena gave a little shriek. 'Keep going, Bennion.'

Bennion had already responded to Annabel. Mrs da Susa didn't spare the car a glance as it cruised past. She was striding out purposefully, face harshly set and a little eerie in the shifting lamplight; a figure tall for a woman and gaunt; the gauntness emphasized by the unbuttoned dark coat, hastily flung on, that flapped about her. Her shoulders were thrust forward, arms working urgently. Annabel peeped out of the rear window and saw her turn into the entrance to Lord Willoughby's.

'Could you pull in, please, Mr Bennion?' Annabel's voice was suddenly taut with excitement.

'Pull in, Bennion,' ordered Sheena.

Annabel was out of the car the moment it stopped and Kate followed. Sheena and Miles made to get out too but Annabel held up her hand. 'Number Two and I will handle this,' she commanded. 'Both Number Threes remain here on guard.'

'Guarding what?' inquired Miles, but Annabel was already speeding away on tiptoe and Kate went after her. She could hear Sheena complaining that there wasn't any point in being a member of the Silent Three if you just hung around in the cold but Miles seemed to be settling happily back in the car. At least they seemed to have accepted their dual role as Number Three.

'They'd just mess everything up again,' Annabel said over her shoulder but she no longer sounded as if she cared. In the entrance to the school grounds they paused, listening. The path to the Band Room, wide enough to take a car, curved darkly ahead between trees. Mrs da Susa had vanished. There was no sound.

'Kate,' whispered Annabel. 'Kate, you remember how the Silent Three story ended?' Annabel's depression had most definitely vanished. Her voice was electric. 'Who the Mystery Man – the gaolbird – turned out to be?'

'He was the Headmistress's brother. They used to have clandestine meetings in a clearing in the school grounds and then they found the loot and –'

'*Clandestine meetings in the school grounds at night, Kate!*'

'Oh, Annabel – you're not suggesting –'

'Then what's she doing here at this time of night?'

'Forgotten something. Coming back to do some work in her study –'

'She wouldn't come to this entrance for that. It only leads to the Band Room. Kate, maybe the missing piece of the jigsaw is fitting into place.'

Annabel set off again, keeping to the grass at the side of the path where the trees provided cover and their footsteps made no sound. The moon was struggling from behind clouds. Suddenly she halted again. Kate had heard the voices, too. Much the louder, raised in anger, was Mrs da Susa's. The other was a barely audible mumble but recognizable as a man's. Standing motionless, listening, Kate was invaded by a feeling of chilling unreality.

'*Raised voices in a clearing,*' murmured Annabel in a strangely vibrant voice, quoting from the picture story. She nudged Kate and they hurried silently forward till the trees came to an end and they could go no further without emerging from cover. But it was far enough.

Between them and the Band Room, in the middle of the path where it was overhung by one lone tree,

Mrs da Susa was in angry confrontation with a man. His back was towards them but it was without doubt the Mystery Man. He was wearing a cherry-red pullover and was of a smallish, jaunty stature, the jauntiness apparent even now when he was cowed under a verbal attack from Mrs da Susa. She had stopped shouting but was hissing at him venomously in an undertone.

In his hand was a suitcase and a bicycle lay on the ground nearby. As Annabel and Kate watched, fascinated, the moon emerged.

'*Falling out over the loot,*' breathed Annabel.

Then behind them they heard footsteps coming along the drive from the direction of Apsley Road. Without speaking they squeezed themselves behind a tree to watch the approach of the new arrival.

It was Julia, hobbling along holding her side and breathing in noisy gasps. She looked anxious as well as exhausted. Emerging from the trees she halted as she saw Mrs da Susa and the Mystery Man who were now invisible to Annabel and Kate because of their position behind the tree.

'Who's that?' they heard Mrs da Susa cry out, sharply.

'It's me, Julia Channing.' Julia sounded fearful. In reply, Mrs da Susa's voice was searing.

'What are you doing here, Julia? Come here.'

Julia shuffled reluctantly forward.

'*Mavis come to report that the Silent Three has got the key!*' hissed Annabel. '*She's going to be in trouble.*'

Apparently so, for Mrs da Susa's voice was again

raised not merely in anger this time, but in a violent tirade in which the name 'Julia' frequently featured. Even in this extraordinary situation it was music to Annabel's ears and she risked a peep round the tree, then stiffened.

'Kate, do you know who the mystery man is?' Annabel was beside herself. With the arrival of Julia the Mystery Man had changed position and his face was now clearly visible. *'Kate, it's her husband. Mr da Susa. Not her brother but a husband's much the same thing –'*

Annabel broke off. There was a new sound. This time it was the gentle purr of an engine turning into the school grounds from the Apsley Road. She listened, disbelieving, as if this were too much even for her.

'Kate, it's incredible. It's happening again, just as it happened at St Babs. You remember how the story ended . . . ? How the villains made up their quarrel and locked the whole school in the dining-hall and then took off from the school playing fields in a light aeroplane with the loot? The Silent Three only foiled them in the nick of time by driving a motor mower across the path of the plane –'

'That can't be an aeroplane, Annabel. An aeroplane wouldn't be able to get along the path. The wings –'

Such details were not for Annabel. For her, St Babs and its strange tale lived and breathed again here in the grounds of Lord Willoughby's. Kate herself, peering from behind the tree, wasn't immune from the feeling. All the leading players in the drama were now gathered together as if for a grand climax. All, including Annabel and herself, were motionless, listening intently to that approaching engine. There was a frozen quality about them as if drawn by an artist and Kate suddenly knew what it felt like to be a line drawing. The whole tableau ought surely to be the last picture, the curtain, to an instalment in a serial story in a comic.

But no. Not quite the last. It wasn't quite dramatic enough for a curtain. It needed one more picture.

Annabel supplied it. Her excitement and sense of the dramatic had been pushed too far to be restrained any longer. Every detail of this mystery had in her mind now satisfactorily locked into place. With one bound she was out from behind the tree and in a striking pose.

In one hand she again held the key high above her head. The other she flung out commandingly, accusingly, with extended forefinger, at the astounded trio. The moonlight fell upon her robes, her hood and mask, bathing them in sinister splendour.

'You are foiled,' she cried, ringingly, 'foiled by the Silent Three!'

It was, thought Kate, a splendid curtain. Exactly right. She almost saw the words hanging from Annabel's mouth in a speech balloon.

But what would the final instalment bring?

Chapter 8

✶✶✶✶✶

The rear of the Franks-Walters' limousine, the source of the engine noise, came into view as it reversed down the path and then halted. A window slid down and a hooded and masked head stuck itself out.

'I'm going home,' it said, snottily, to the first other hooded figure it saw which happened to be Annabel who had just lowered her arms with deliberate and magnificent slowness. 'I'm not going to sit here like a lemon all night. If you didn't want me why didn't you say so instead of being a couple of old head-in-sanders. The other Number Three's coming as well. I'm dropping him off.'

Kate could see Miles bouncing happily up and down on the seat beside her. His idealism hadn't lasted long, once in contact with the Franks-Walters' life-style.

Sheena suddenly remembered something. 'By the way, Julia Channing was looking for you. I told her you'd come up here.'

On this disconcerting note she was about to withdraw her head into the car when it dawned upon her that there was more to the situation then had at first met her eye. She glanced round and saw Mrs da Susa and her companions, still frozen in attitudes of disbelief at this further development. Her eyes bulged through the mask.

Just then the lid of Mr da Susa's suitcase, which had been insecurely fastened, fell open with a thump.

Despite everything; her grave doubts as to whether Annabel was on the right track, her feelings of confusion at the course which events had taken; despite it all Kate knew then only one desire – to know what was inside. Could it be – was it possible – conceivable – that from it would pour a cascade of glittering gems . . . ?

The contents tumbled out in a kind of slow motion.

It was a large and rickety model ship. Kate could tell it was rickety even at that distance because it was falling apart before it hit the ground. The masts struck first and shattered.

There came a scream of anguish from Mr da Susa. He gazed for a long moment at his ruined model and then, bending his knees and addressing the heavens with his fists, he launched into a cascade of glittering Italian in front of his visibly shaken wife. The sight was so fascinating that Kate forgot caution and stepped out from behind the tree to watch, Miles Noggins stuck his head out of the far side of the car and even Bennion looked round. Annabel remained motionless.

Having exhausted Italian, Mr da Susa turned to English. For this he needed an audience and he cared not that the only available one was a motley collection of hooded and masked figures, a chauffeur and a

Band Room Monitor. Lowering his arms he addressed them, emphasizing each point by stabbing his forefinger down at the broken model.

'This,' he yelled, 'is a very bossy woman. I try to make my model at home and she kicks me out because I am making the mess. So I am reduced to becoming the thief and stealing the keys to the Band Room and sneaking in there in the evenings and then what happens? Just as I finish she comes to kick me out of there, too, and now smash! My model is smash! It was my entry for the Arca competition. It is a *very*, *very*, *very* bossy woman.'

Having said which, he took a flying kick at the model which sailed into the air with bits falling off it and landed in the bamboo clumps.

The sympathies of his audience were with him and Annabel and Kate, in particular, were entirely in agreement. But they had problems of their own.

This revelation that the Mystery Man, *alias* Mr da Susa, was not an ex-gaolbird looking for stolen loot but merely one of the underprivileged, so sympathized with by Mrs da Susa, who had need of the Band Room in which to express themselves because of unsatisfactory home conditions, had demolished at one stroke the whole Deep Game theory. It lay as much in ruins as did Mr da Susa's model.

True, there remained the Great Injustice and the mystery of why Julia had been secretly searching for a key in the school grounds at night but obviously a quiet re-think was required.

To do Julia justice which one had to, however reluctantly, it was now plain that she had had good

cause for believing that it was Charlie Ash who had
been getting into the Band Room in the evenings.
Mr da Susa had been engaged in the same occu-
pation, making the same sort of mess, that Charlie
had.

It was time to go away and review the situation.

Annabel stepped briskly over to the car and
opened the door.

'Move over,' she said to Sheena. 'Come on, Kate.'
The door slammed shut.

'Would you mind stepping on it, please, Mr
Bennion?' said Annabel.

'Step on it, Bennion,' ordered Sheena.

*

Julia was waiting at the gates when Annabel and
Kate arrived at school next morning, their robes in
their schoolbags. They both had a morning-after-the-
night-before feeling and were nervous about what
the day had in store for them but the sight of Julia
revived them. She looked as if she hadn't slept and
she was cringing and fawning as she came forward to
meet them.

'Please, Annabel,' she was very agitated, 'please
let me have the key.'

'Key?' said Annabel. 'What key?'

'Oh, Annabel, you know perfectly well what key.
The one you were waving outside my window last
night. I ran all the way to school after you to ask for
it back.'

'Last night? What's she talking about, Kate? Do
you know?'

'I think, Annabel, she might be confusing you with that organization called the Silent Three. I did hear they were about last night. I'm only guessing, though.'

'Ah! The Silent Three. Then you've come to the right person, Julia, because we've got some influence there, I think, haven't we Kate. But you'll have to tell us what all this is about if you want us to help. What is this key?'

'It's the key to the store-room in the Band Room. You know it is, Annabel.'

Not by any twitch or flicker did Annabel reveal her disappointment.

'How did you come to lose that, Julia?'

'Annabel, you're torturing me. You know we've always been friends. Doesn't our friendship mean anything to you?'

'But how, Julia?'

'I think it must have dropped out of my pocket when I was doing somersaults on that big branch in the grounds and then when I went back to look for it Mr Rumator had dug the ground over and it must have got buried. Did it get buried, Annabel? Is that where you – is that where it got found?'

'You were doing somersaults on the branch with the First Years, were you, Julia? That doesn't sound very dignified for a Band Room Monitor. Cabinet Ministers don't do somersaults on branches, do they.'

Julia's eyes filled with tears and she started babbling.

'Oh, Annabel, it's been awful. I didn't dare tell

anybody I'd lost it because Mrs da Susa warned me I mustn't because the spare keys had disappeared and it was the only one and I had to go out at night digging for it and still I couldn't find it and there's things locked up in the store-room like the table tennis equipment and there's a chess set belonging to a boy called Charlie Ash –'

'That's the chess set you confiscated, isn't it, Julia.'

'I didn't really confiscate it, Annabel. I just had to say that because I couldn't tell anybody I'd lost the key. He can have it back as soon as I can get the door open. He'd left it in there.'

Annabel sighed and looked melancholy for a moment.

'Of course, Mrs da Susa's got the spare keys back now,' said Julia. 'Her husband had them. But they're in her study and I – well, I suppose I might as well tell you. I'm not Band Room Monitor any more.'

'Oh?'

'Mrs da Susa informed me last night. She shouted it rather loudly in fact – perhaps you heard but then if you're not the Silent Three you wouldn't have. She was angry because I interrupted her in the middle of a row with her husband and then I had to tell her what I was doing there … it was all the Silent Three's fault really because if they hadn't appeared and I hadn't gone chasing after them it wouldn't all have happened …

'But, anyway, she still wants my key back. She ordered me to find it by today.'

'I'll make a bargain with you, Julia,' said Annabel.

'I use my influence with the Silent Three to get your key back if you agree to bring Charlie Ash's chess set to me straight afterwards. I'll have the key left under a stone outside the Band Room door by morning break.'

Julia clasped her hands.

'Oh, Annabel, of course I'll agree. Annabel, I shall always be your true friend. If you're ever in need of help just turn to me –'

'We'll be late for Assembly,' said Kate.

Stripped of her recent authority, Julia now looked a piteous, pathetic, cringing figure. Annabel regarded her quite kindly for a moment. 'There, there,' she said, patting her on the forearm, and then she and Kate moved on.

'The Silent Three did a bit of good then,' observed Kate as they made their way into Assembly. 'It got rid of Julia as Band Room Monitor.'

'A bit of good? A *lot* of good!' retorted Annabel spiritedly. But she still hadn't recovered from her bitter disappointment over the key.

The last mystery was resolved. All they were waiting for now, thought Kate, were the repercussions.

*

There were no repercussions. Later that morning, at break, Mrs da Susa sat at her desk with an open comic in front of her reviewing the extraordinary events of the previous evening and trying to analyse where she had gone wrong. How had she, Mrs da

Susa, modern, enlightened, highly qualified, intelligent – she had excellent degrees to prove it – managed to conjure up, at her school, such scenes from an old comic?

It had all been a considerable shock, and no doubt several charges of breaches of school discipline could be levelled against the hooded and masked figures involved. However, she had taken no action and didn't intend to. There were various reasons for this, not all of them cowardly.

True, of course, the circumstances *were* embarrassing. It would be undesirable to have to dwell on the fact that, as the hooded figures now knew, her husband had been trespassing on school property, having stolen the Band Room keys from her study at school, and that he had been making a mess there.

Undesirable, too, to have the news spread about the school that she and Salvatore had had an undignified and violent quarrel in which silly things had been said. Better to keep the temperature low by turning a blind eye to the misdemeanours which, since they apparently had as a root cause Julia Channing's stewardship of the Band Room, would presumably not now recur.

There was, too, the slightly embarrassing matter of having lost her temper with Julia Channing and screaming at her, in that old phrase of her mother's, like an old fishwife.

To be fair to herself, she had been under strain from the moment when it had dawned upon her where Salvatore might be disappearing to in the evenings. She had been pondering again the mystery of the missing Band Room keys when she had suddenly remembered the cloud of sawdust that had risen from his trousers when she picked them up for the wash that morning from where he had left them in the customary place, thrown on the bedroom floor. She had put two and two together and stormed intemperately off to investigate and had found him just leaving the Band Room.

And now, having been forced into a feeling of guilt over their quarrel, she was going to have to pay for it. At breakfast he had cheerfully told her he was giving up model-making. There was, in the paper, an advert for a quantity of photographic equipment, going cheap. It would mean turning the bathroom into a dark-room but it was an opportunity not to be missed. She had replied: 'Yes, Salvatore, dear.'

Far overshadowing any of that, however, was the fact that Mrs da Susa felt that she, as Head – Deputy Head – must herself take the blame for all that had happened. She had been only too ready to hold Miss Sterndale to account for the appalling events at St Babs. In all justice, then, she must now apply the same harsh strictures to herself.

She had clearly been wrong to appoint Julia Channing Band Room Monitor. The girl had simply not been up to it. Her achievements in her brief tenure of office had been to empty the place with amazing rapidity, to lose the only available key to the store-room and to inspire the formation of a secret organization dedicated to her overthrow.

(True, Julia had now returned the key. She had brought it to Mrs da Susa's study door only a few minutes ago, blushing and stammering some incomprehensible explanation about heaven-knew-what. But the key was by now almost incidental.)

From today, the Band Room would resume life without a monitor. She, Mrs da Susa, was going to have to try to keep out of Mrs Channing's way for some time. It wasn't going to be easy but there was no alternative. She, Mrs da Susa again, had failed.

She turned the pages of her comic, this time regarding the Headmistress of St Babs with considerably more sympathy than before; indeed, with some fellow feeling. She felt she would like to have had a chat with her. A particular picture of Miss Sterndale caught her eye. She was gazing powerfully out at the reader from under knitted brows and saying: 'I am baffled! Baffled as to what to do about the Silent Three!' Mrs da Susa nodded knowingly.

There, too, was Mavis, the resemblance to Julia as remarkable as ever. She looked, it occurred to Mrs da Susa before she could prevent the thought entering her head, a pain in the neck.

To rid herself of such unenlightened ideas she rose, carrying her comic and went to the window. The real Julia immediately swam before her eyes. She was walking past, looking much better than she had only a few minutes ago when she had brought the key back. Indeed, for someone who had not long ago been sacked in ignominious circumstances, she appeared remarkably full of herself.

Julia was, in fact, already adjusting. Being Band Room Monitor hadn't in practice been a lot of fun. After the first heady flush it had proved more of a nerve-racking responsibility. But to have *been* Band Room Monitor ... dismissed merely because of unlucky circumstances ... ah! that was a glory to look back on for ever. Together with the sure knowledge of being gifted but misunderstood ...

Watching her, Mrs da Susa had a momentary desire, also quickly suppressed, to push her in the swimming-pool.

She was about to turn away when a rather small boy came into view. It was Charlie Ash of the First Year, an odd child, she always thought. He was walking very slowly and holding in one hand a wooden box from which he was taking various objects and examining them. It looked to be a chess set.

Suddenly he closed the box and, with a look of infinite happiness, started to skip. Each bound higher than the last, legs crossing each other, he skipped away till he was lost from view.

Frowning slightly at the childishness of his behaviour, Mrs da Susa returned to her desk.

Where had she gone wrong? What ought she to have done?

★

Mrs da Susa was looking back on her failure. In the boiler room that evening the four members of the Silent Three gathered for the last time round the candle flame as their leader, Number One, prepared to report complete success. Before beginning she looked at each masked face and thanked them in turn for their loyalty and devotion. 'Numbers 2, 3 A and 3 B,' – the new numbers were now daubed on their hoods – 'it is these qualities that have brought us our triumph.'

She glanced at the paper in her hand, holding it near the candle flame.

'First and most important – the Great Injustice. This morning Julia Channing brought to me Charlie Ash's chess set, as agreed, and I returned it to him. The wrong has been righted and the vile tyrant humbled. She is no longer Band Room Monitor. I propose that we now consider the slate wiped clean, the Silent Three being an organization that tempers justice with mercy.'

'Hear, hear!' put in Number 3 B.

'Second – the Deep Game. We have succeeded in proving that there wasn't one – on this occasion.'

Number One paused and glanced round once more at each of her companions. When she spoke again there was a note of regret in her voice.

'The tale of St Babs was a spectacular saga of evil, treachery and corruption. About St Babs I have to say there was a certain *grandeur*. At Willers there has just been a lot of muddle and confusion.'

She sighed, and there was a still deeper note of regret in the sigh.

'For the moment our work is finished save for passing on to you Charlie Ash's grateful thanks and expressing our hope that his chess set will do well in the Arca competition . . .' – 'Hear, Hear!' said Number 3 A – '. . . We can now put away our robes and masks. But I know that you, fellow members of the Silent Three, stand ready as I do to don them once more when the call comes again to fight for justice.'

She bowed her head and there was silence. The candle flame spluttered and leapt.

'Now I think it's supper time, Number Two. We've got steak and kidney pie tonight.'

They removed their robes and masks for the last time and gave them to Sheena to take home. Then they dispersed, Numbers One and Two walking back home together along Church Lane.

Charlie Ash's chess set came second in the Arca competition.

Annabel and the rotten things of life

*****

Chapter 1

*****

It wasn't often that Annabel or Kate allowed thoughts of Addendon Town Council to cross their minds. It was an institution of little interest, a vague body spending its time in violent squabbles about matters over which it seemed to have no control anyway. COUNCIL GIVES FIRM THUMBS-DOWN TO ROAD-WIDENING SCHEME, the *Advertiser* would scream. Soon afterwards the widening would begin. COUNCIL WELCOMES PERMANENT SITE FOR GYPSIES. No such site would ever appear.

For the town council had few real powers. On anything considered important it could only make recommendations to the bodies that did have the power, usually the district council. Mostly these recommendations appeared to be ignored but this never inhibited councillors from fighting each other tooth and nail over them.

All this normally concerned Annabel very little. Why then, on that pleasant Wednesday evening, was she walking towards the Memorial Hall where the monthly meeting of the town council was due to begin at 8 o'clock? Why was she stern of face and holding in her right hand some pages torn from an exercise book and covered closely with handwriting, looking for all the world as if she were about to make a speech?

Why, in brief, and particularly on an evening such as this, ideal for playing tennis or a dozen other lovely things, was she taking the town council seriously? A few paces behind her as she entered the hall came Kate, looking sheepish.

In the centre of the hall a long table awaited the councillors. It was not yet quite five to eight and so far only two of the chairs were occupied, one by the Mayor (or chairman, or chair, depending upon who was referring to him; his title alone could lead to squabbles) Mr Cantrill; the other, immediately to his right, by the Town Clerk, Mr Poynton-Green.

Both were visibly surprised to see who was entering. Elderly, leanly stooping, leather-faced, gentlemanly Mr Cantrill adjusted his glasses for a keener stare. Mr Poynton-Green rose languidly to his feet and, murmuring something about 'not enough chairs for members of the public' started looking vaguely around the room, finally producing two fold-up chairs from a cupboard which he opened out and plonked down for Annabel and Kate without much grace before handing each an agenda. Annabel thanked him somewhat coldly and they sat down. It seemed that members of the public were not given a warm welcome.

The only other member of the public present, now gazing at them, was none other than Mr Ribbons, their Far Left Wing physics teacher. He awarded them a brief nod. He was in fact the only regular attender at town council meetings; for what purpose who could tell? Possibly merely studying effete democracy in action: possibly plotting its violent overthrow.

Mr Poynton-Green resumed his seat and Annabel began glancing through her notes. She looked tense, lips moving as she murmured to herself. Kate shifted in her seat uneasily, watching the councillors as one by one they arrived for the meeting, in almost every case casting surprised glances towards the unusually full public gallery. Kate avoided their eyes.

The arrival of Mrs Winnie Stringer, bustling in with a cheerful 'good evening' to everyone, reminded Kate of the only previous occasion when Annabel had taken an interest in the town council. It had been one of those rare occasions when the council had actually taken a decision and acted upon it, an event which invariably led to trouble. On this occasion it had been the filling in of a little pond called Woozy's Pond which had infuriated Annabel and a lot of other people besides.

It had been filled in on the grounds that it was a safety hazard to small children and was unhealthy, unsightly and smelly. All this had been ridiculed by opponents who pointed out that it had been there since time immemorial and hadn't killed or injured anyone so far as was known. Annabel, like others, thought it was lovely and had a nice pondy, weedy smell.

The prime mover behind the pond-filling episode had been Mrs Stringer which was perhaps surprising since, although the generally held view of her as a self-important windbag was absolutely correct, she did have the saving grace, to Annabel's eyes at any rate, of having a soft spot for old Addendon and of fighting for it.

It was simply that whenever such key words as *child safety*, *health hazard*, *compassion* – particularly *compassion* – were introduced into an issue, such rational judgement as she possessed instantly foundered and she was at the mercy of anyone who produced such trump cards.

Accordingly, when an indignant young mother had come to see her to complain that her Gareth, aged four, had come home howling and muddy-legged after falling into the pond near their new house while fishing for tadpoles, and to go on to demand that the pond be filled in because it was dangerous to children (and where questions of *child safety* were concerned anyone of *compassion* must surely respond) and that she also thought the pond a *health hazard* because it was so smelly besides being unsightly . . . well, it had all been too much for Mrs Stringer and she had hurled herself into verbose action. For weeks the *Advertiser* had smelt of the pond. Only when it was all over, after Mrs Stringer had bored and bulldozed the other councillors into submission, the decision taken and the pond filled in, had she paused to wonder, in the quiet of her Mill Lane home where the stillness was broken only by the soothing snores of her husband in his armchair, whether she herself had wanted this nice little pond filled in: particularly as little Gareth was now apparently howling because there was no longer anywhere to fish for tadpoles.

But whatever else the decision had been, it had been a triumph of decisiveness. Something had been achieved, if only negatively. It had been a heady period.

Kate wondered now if the pond episode featured in the notes which Annabel was frowning over. Probably.

The table was filling up, the last councillors taking their seats. There was, Kate noticed, an undercurrent of expectancy, even excitement. Was the meeting going to discuss something of especial interest?

She glanced at the agenda she had been given. Oh, yes. The main item concerned the forthcoming visit to Addendon of the local television company. They were running a weekly series of Saturday morning programmes called *Live From* . . . , featuring small towns in the region and their problems, and on the coming Saturday it was Addendon's turn. *Live From Addendon* was to be presented by Mrs Stringer, no less, and the problem to be featured was the controversial Birdbath Issue.

Kate had almost forgotten about that row. It had been going on for years. The birdbath was to have been erected as Addendon's contribution to the celebrations of the birth of Prince William. Prince William was now growing up and still his birdbath wasn't in place in Addendon, Kate couldn't remember for what reason.

But no wonder that Mrs Stringer, in particular, was looking so excited. Kate nudged Annabel and pointed out the item to her but Annabel wasn't interested.

She was growing more and more restive. The meeting was beginning. Mr Poynton-Green read out the apologies for absence and then the minutes of the previous meeting. There followed various nit-picking suggestions for alterations to the minutes, mainly from Mrs Stringer, while Annabel rolled her eyes impatiently and muttered to herself. At one point she almost rose to her feet then decided against it.

After the minutes had been approved there were reports to be made and correspondence to be read out, most of it fiercely insulting to the council, but councillors were used to this and heard it through indulgently.

Annabel's impatience was by now hardly containable, so much so that at one point Mr Cantrill halted the meeting to request members of the public to restrain from fidgeting since councillors found if very distracting when they were trying to concentrate upon weighty matters of public concern. Councillors nodded their agreement.

Annabel continued to bob up and down in her seat, however, and Kate slumped lower and lower in hers and waited for the inevitable.

It came just as the council reached the item they had all been waiting for. Mr Cantrill invited Mrs Stringer, in her dual role of Chairperson of the Television Broadcast Sub-committee and Chairperson of the Commemorative Birdbath Sub-committee, to speak. Councillors shifted in their seats and perked up.

Kate noticed that there was one exception to this. Mr Poynton-Green was thoughtfully writing in his notebook. Or possibly he was doodling. The movement of his hand was slow and repetitive as if shading something in. At any rate he didn't appear to be sharing in the general enthusiasm. He looked merely pensive.

At this point Annabel lost patience for she knew that if Mrs Stringer were invited to speak she would do so for hours. It was time they got down to important matters. Annabel had come here determined to address the council and it could be delayed no longer, for it was getting perilously close to bedtime and her mother would be expecting her back. It was all right for these councillors. They could stay up till midnight and they didn't have homework. She and Mrs Stringer rose simultaneously.

Mrs Stringer, flushed with pleasure, had just managed to get out: 'Mr Chairman, as we all know, the television broadcast is almost upon us –' when there was a commotion behind her.

'Mr Chairperson,' cried Annabel. 'I wish to address the council.'

A hush fell. Every rustling paper and scraping chair and cough was suddenly stilled. Mrs Stringer, open-mouthed and quivering, turned and glared.

'I wish,' cried Annabel, now that she had everyone's attention, 'to speak about the rotten things of life.'

Uproar! Protestations from councillors! Annabel

ignored them. She drew a deep breath, glanced at her notes and prepared to launch into her speech. Above the noise came the stern voice of Mr Cantrill.

'I must ask members of the public to sit down. Members of the public are not allowed to speak at council meetings.'

'I am talking in particular,' shrieked Annabel determinedly, 'about the tree in Addendon Rec that you want to cut down.'

'The council will now go into secret session,' roared Mr Cantrill. 'The Clerk will see to it that the room is cleared.'

Annabel and Kate found themselves being escorted through the door. Mr Ribbons was leaving too but he didn't seem to mind. He looked as if he had had a little revolutionary thrill. And it wasn't every day that you could get a little revolutionary thrill in Addendon.

Chapter 2

*****

All this had arisen because of the tree in Addendon Recreation Ground. Annabel was very fond of trees, not least because they were the homes of so many creatures. This one was a special favourite, a huge and ancient oak made still more majestic by its battle-scars, for it had the air, so Annabel maintained, of a wounded warrior.

At some point in its centuries-long career, one side of it had been shattered by lightning and although it had recovered valiantly the experience had left it with a lop-sided look. The bark had been stripped away down one side and a great decaying wound was eating its way into the tree, slowly hollowing it out. The wound was an absorbing little world in its own right, rich in fungi and lichens and interesting little holes and crevices.

Some of the branches were dying and any wind brought down a litter of dead wood, though it was too decayed and light to do harm even if it were to hit anyone, which it never did. The litter lay strewn about beneath the tree, rotting moistly and sprouting toadstools of its own.

It was an old soldier of a tree, a sylvan Chelsea Pensioner, its great crooked branches as thick as the trunks of lesser trees. It was also a marvellous tree to climb if you didn't mind heights. Annabel wasn't keen on them herself but she'd braved it once and come down exhilarated saying that it would be wonderful to have a tree-house up there because there were such splendidly green and secret hidey-holes among the branches. It was more fun than the Adventure Playground installed by the council on the other side of the Rec.

It was, too, home to countless creatures, mostly insects but including squirrels, a pair of green wood-peckers and, Annabel believed, a tawny owl which used to hoot around the Rec after dark. Annabel liked them all, even the wood-lice.

So it had been a shock, walking through the Rec one day, to see Mr Crick standing looking at the tree. For Mr Crick was the best-known tree surgeon around Addendon and got all the council business. His intentions were plain from the way in which, while rolling a cigarette with one hand and licking it, he was idly eyeing the line of fall and glancing around and upwards to make sure there were no obstructions.

Annabel hastened over to him. 'You're not going to cut it down, are you!' she said in disbelief.

The end of his cigarette flared into flame as he lit it, reducing it to half its original size. He looked at her and, being a taciturn man, merely nodded.

'Why?'

'Council wants it down. Some of it's rotten. It's got woodworm in it, look.'

'Is it going to fall down?'

'Fall down?' He puffed out his breath in a *pah* of

derision, causing the remaining tobacco in his cigarette to blow out. 'See my son out as well as me. His son too, I expect.'

'Then what do they want to cut it down for?'

'Better ask them. I know they're going to plant some flowering cherries in its place. I think they think it makes the place untidy. Too much dead wood falling down and getting in the way of the mower and that. I think they had some sort of complaint as well. Personally I like it, but then I'm sentimental about trees.'

'You're not sawing it down right now, are you?'

'Oh, no. I'm just taking a look for to give Mr Poynton-Green a quote. I shan't do nothing for a week or two.'

He went off towards his van which was parked nearby, an amiable, hunch-shouldered, plodding figure in green overalls, licking another cigarette paper and working out his quote.

But all Annabel saw was the Grim Reaper.

*

It threw Annabel into despair and brought out all her protective instincts. She loved that tree; loved it more than she had ever known until now.

'It's always the same, Kate. We don't appreciate things till they're threatened. I'll never want to go in the Rec again if they cut that down. It'd be like cutting down Grandpa.'

Kate tried to comfort her.

'There are lots of other trees, Annabel. Thousands of them just around Addendon.'

'That, Kate, is like saying: "There are millions of people. What's it matter if you lose a friend?"'

'After all, Annabel, flowering cherries are very pretty.'

'In their place, Kate, but not there. You can't replace a tree like that with some silly little flowering cherries. Anyway, what good's a flowering cherry to a woodpecker or an owl? What good is it to a wood-louse?'

But it was when Kate suggested, timidly, that the tree was, after all, decaying that Annabel became most impassioned.

'Kate, how could you? I *like* things that are rotten and decaying. I *love* them. I don't like things that are shiny and new, except for clothes, of course, and Christmas presents. I love decaying old roofs and houses and streets and rotting old logs with beetles crawling out of them and toadstools and smelly old ponds and rank old grass and faded old cafés – faded old anything, come to that. These, Kate, are some of my favourite things.

'And then there are all the little creatures that feed off rotten things and the creatures that live on them. Decay is part of life, Kate. I hate things that don't rot. I am, Kate, a student of decay, a devotee of rot.'

Her lip trembled.

'I shan't let them do it, Kate.'

*

Normally Annabel might have had some success at least in stirring up a fuss since people do care about trees, but in this case it seemed to have got about that the tree was rotten and its felling therefore inevitable. 'It'll have to come down some-time,' people said, shrugging.

Annabel had insisted on going to the council meeting although Kate had warned her they wouldn't let her address them. And now, what next, if anything?

'We could try seeing some of the town councillors separately,' said Annabel, as they went home. 'Or there's Mr Poynton-Green. He's the Clerk, the one that's giving Mr Crick the orders. Maybe we could persuade him. He usually looks a bit more cheerful than the others.'

But she herself sounded, most unusually for her, dispirited and depressed. It was, Kate supposed, an inevitable reaction. Annabel had been hoping for so much from her speech, had worked so hard on it; and then she hadn't been allowed even to start it. As they passed a litter bin on a lamp post, Kate noticed Annabel quietly crumple up her pages of notes and drop them in.

Addendon Town Council had broken many brave spirits in the past. Internally feuding it might be but let an outsider criticize and it closed ranks and became as a brick wall, impervious to persuasion or reason or changing its views. What chance did Annabel have, alone but for Kate? None. Absolutely, utterly, positively and without question: none.

Nevertheless, on the following evening they walked down the Corton Compton Road to Mr

Poynton-Green's semi-detached house and rang the doorbell. Kate noticed when he appeared that, as at the council meeting, he wasn't looking his normal cheerful self.

Mr Poynton-Green was, in fact, nursing a worry of his own; a very large, very secret worry.

*

Mr D. E. Poynton-Green (Derek to his friends) was a familiar figure around Addendon. Handsome and urbane, a little smile usually playing about his lips, he was often to be seen strolling about, always well-dressed whether in hacking jacket and cavalry twill or lounge suit and slightly flamboyant bow tie. Frequently he swung a stick or umbrella.

A stranger might have found it difficult to guess his profession. Something successful in the arts, possibly? An actor? (He was, as it happens, a leading member of the Addendon Players.) Barrister? Or – and this was perhaps what he most conveyed and what gave him his dangerous charm – a playboy who, having made a fortune by gambling, had inexplicably chosen Addendon in which to settle down and spend it.

In fact, he was a clerk in an insurance company in Querminster. He had been in the same job ever since leaving school without being promoted because he was bone idle and lacked powers of concentration. It was irksome to have to sit at a row of desks with other clerks twenty years his junior but he was too lazy to do anything about it, and fortunately the desire for power which lurked within his breast could be satisfied by his part-time position as Clerk to the Addendon Town Council.

This power was greater than might have appeared. True, apart from a few small matters the council's authority was limited to the making of recommendations. But councillors took these recommendations very seriously. Passions could run high and sometimes councillors would quiver with rage and abuse each other. Mrs Stringer was usually prominent in these deliberations for her voice had a quality of unstoppability that the chairman found hard to control.

Mr Poynton-Green, whose job it was to take the minutes and carry out the instructions of the council once a vote had been taken, would sit and listen to these debates with an appearance of keen and efficient, though of course dispassionate, interest as he apparently made notes for the minutes.

In fact, he was doodling. It was far too much effort to try to make sense out of all that shouting and argument. Much easier to think up a few lines later. And if it were all wrong, so what! Nobody else would remember it very clearly anyway.

As for carrying out the council's instructions, well, he would smile courteously, nod, then go off and do exactly as he felt like. Sometimes he wouldn't take any action at all. Taking action probably meant writing a letter or several letters. The council was too mean to give him a secretary and typing was a laborious, two-fingered business better avoided if possible. His philosophy was that since nobody took much notice of the council anyway it didn't matter whether he sent off their recommendations or not. And nobody would ever find out since councillors never asked to look at the files, which was just as well because mostly there weren't any.

If he had a personal interest in a matter, however, it would be very different. Then he would spring into action, although not necessarily the action the council had instructed him to take. It would be the action which suited his purpose.

Such were the workings of democracy in Addendon. For years, thanks to Mr Poynton-Green, the council's agonized deliberations had for the most part been a pointless waste of time.

But now, perhaps, nemesis was nigh. Mr Poynton-Green, who seldom worried about anything, was suddenly a very worried man. It was the forthcoming television programme, *Live From Addendon*, combined with the controversial birdbath issue, which threatened his exposure.

★

His mind was on other things, therefore, when he received Annabel and Kate on his doorstep. He greeted them courteously and said that in fact he wasn't unsympathetic. However, he had no say in this. It was a council decision which he merely carried out.

In any case, the tree was rotten, wasn't it? (Annabel bridled.) So Mrs Stringer had said, anyway, and she was the one who'd proposed the tree be felled and replaced with flowering cherries. The other councillors had simply gone along with her. She'd been responding to a complaint by a young mother whose child, Andrea or Andrew or something like that, had nearly been struck by a bit of falling branch. She'd said it was a question of child safety.

Kate saw Annabel close her eyes briefly. It was Woozy's Pond all over again.

'What about the wood-lice?' said Annabel, sharply.

'I beg your pardon?'

'The wood-lice and the beetles and all the little creatures that feed on dead wood. What are they supposed to do? They've got a right to life, too.'

Mr Poynton-Green pondered that.

'And then there are the toadstools. The fungi. There are lots of them and they're lovely.'

'There are probably lots of fungi,' replied Mr Poynton-Green, in a rather smarty, know-all manner, 'because the wood's dead.'

'But the fungi aren't.'

Mr Poynton-Green pondered that, too.

'Even a fungus,' added Annabel, bitterly, 'has a right to live. It may not do anything except absorb food but you could say that about some human beings.'

Mr Poynton-Green, who was spending the evening having dinner and sitting in an armchair, did not wish to be drawn into aimless philosophizing.

'I'm sorry,' he said, 'but there's really no point in discussing it with me. I suggest you go and see Mrs Stringer.'

E.M.A.—6

As they left, he said: 'By the way, Mr Crick intends felling the tree on Saturday morning so I'm afraid you haven't much time left.'

The spirit seemed to have gone out of Annabel entirely. They trudged in silence to Mill Lane but it was only to learn that Mrs Stringer wasn't at home anyway. Her husband seemed to think she might be at home on the following evening, probably preparing for her television broadcast. Annabel was low all next day. Kate had never known her like it. In the evening they returned to Mill Lane to try Mrs Stringer again, but as it happened they couldn't have called at a worse time.

Mrs Stringer had a television director with her. He'd come to Addendon to make final preparations for the following morning's programme and as Mrs Stringer attempted to charm him over a cup of tea the very last thing she wanted to see through her window was the garden gate opening to admit Annabel Fidelity Bunce.

At the time, she and the director were discussing the birdbath issue which was to be the main feature of the programme.

*

The birdbath issue was, Mrs Stringer believed, a simple though sadly typical case of a democratic decision by the town council being overruled by a dictatorial and unfeeling District.

In fact, it wasn't quite like that.

The council had voted to have the birdbath erected in honour of the birth of Prince William, and as a site for it Mrs Stringer had proposed the tiny open space outside Mr Poynton-Green's house on the Corton Compton Road. There was a little-used bench seat there and Mrs Stringer's idea had been that the seat might be more used, particularly by the elderly, if there were the attraction of being able to watch the birds bathing from it.

The council had enthusiastically agreed and instructed Mr Poynton-Green to obtain the necessary approval from the district council.

There had been consternation when, subsequently, Mr Poynton-Green had reported that permission had been refused on the grounds that the birdbath would form an obstruction on the grass verge, the district council suggesting it be sited instead on the Recreation Ground.

After making his report, Mr Poynton-Green had leaned back in his chair in his usual urbane manner, only to sit smartly upright again when, instead of his report being tamely accepted as he had expected, Mrs Stringer had risen, red with rage, to say that this time District had gone too far. Sweeping her fellow councillors along with her she had insisted that they stand and fight. The Clerk must write back, challenging the decision.

What Mrs Stringer hadn't known and still didn't know was that Mr Poynton-Green hadn't contacted the district council at all. Whilst all Mr Poynton-Green knew was that he didn't want a lot of people sitting watching birds bathing outside his house and he had accordingly made up a suitably worded refusal purporting to come from the district council, assuming that councillors would accept it in their normal docile manner.

He had now been faced with having to concoct a wholly fictitious correspondence in which the district council remained firm. And then just when, with the passing of the years, the town council was coming round, albeit with much grumbling, to accept that the birdbath would have to go in the Rec, along had come the television company stirring the whole thing up again.

Mr Poynton-Green was now awaiting the programme with dread. The district council was normally a remote body, dealt with by correspondence or telephone, but inevitably someone from there would see the programme and learn for the first time of the birdbath issue and their supposed dictatorial role in it. His long, buccaneering record of running the town council his way must surely be exposed and he was now spending sleepless nights trying to summon up the courage to confess and resign without being quite able to bring himself to do so.

Mrs Stringer, of course, knew nothing of this. Her overwhelming interest at this moment was that the following morning would see her television debut; one large step forward to fame and a wider political stage.

This quiet, fringe-bearded young director (the real purpose of the *Live from* ... series was to give greenhorn directors a chance to mess about and acquire experience cheaply, where they couldn't do much harm) now sipping her tea, held her political future in his hands. And here, interfering again, turning up as if to cue, was Annabel Bunce, no doubt wishing to talk a lot of rubbish.

'There's someone at the door,' observed the quiet young director as the bell chimed melodiously.

'I'm sorry about this,' said Mrs Stringer, peevishly. 'I shan't be more than a moment.'

What happened next was out of character for both Annabel and Mrs Stringer. They were, however, both fraught and obsessed in their different ways.

'I'm sorry,' said Mrs Stringer, while still opening the door. 'I'm extremely busy at the moment. Unless it's something of great importance I'd be grateful if you'd call another time.'

'But it *is* of great importance,' replied Annabel, infiltrating rapidly through the loophole so foolishly supplied. 'Isn't it, Kate.'

Kate, lingering behind her, nodded her agreement.

'I've come,' said Annabel, 'to appeal for the rotten things of life.'

At this point Mrs Stringer lost her head. The most important man in her life so far – and she wasn't forgetting her husband – was waiting in the next room. She tried to close the door.

Seeing this, Annabel lost her head, too. She had reached the end of her tether. She put a foot in the door, then an elbow. Mrs Stringer, now committed, pushed harder. There was a brief struggle and Annabel, seeing herself losing, let out an agonised screech.

'Vandals!' she yelled, giving voice to all her pent-up despair. 'Vandals! It's just like the pond all over again, isn't it, Kate? The vandals filled in the pond and now they want to cut our tree down tomorrow morning.'

This was overheard by the director who peeped cautiously round the door into the hall to see what was going on. For the first time, he began to have hopes of the Addendon programme.

The reference to the pond touched a raw spot and inflamed Mrs Stringer still further. She put her shoulder to the door and with one violent push got it closed. After bolting it as a sensible precaution she returned, panting and quivering, to the sitting-room.

'I'm sorry about the interruption,' she puffed to the director. 'They'd called at the wrong house.'

There was a violent flurry of banging on the knocker and the doorbell chimed again.

'Children!' quivered Mrs Stringer.

From behind her came a loud knocking on glass and when she turned, startled, it was to see a face grimacing at her through the window, a wild, sobbing, despairing face.

'I shall do something desperate. You'll see!' screamed Annabel. And fled.

It could have been, as Mrs Stringer took it at the time, nothing more than a last cry of hopeless fury from someone who had been worsted.

But apparently not. For next morning Annabel had disappeared. Her bed hadn't been slept in and she had left a note.

Chapter 3

*****

Mrs Stringer learnt of it when she rang the Bunces at ten to nine the following morning to smooth things over. She had wakened conscious of having behaved in a regrettably undignified manner on the previous evening. It cast a cloud over the day, particularly when she remembered how talkative the Bunce girl was. Straight after breakfast, therefore, she looked up Bunce in the phone book and rang the number.

The receiver was picked up almost immediately by an agitated-sounding Mrs Bunce.

'She's disappeared,' she said, in a tremulous voice, in response to Mrs Stringer's request to speak to Annabel. 'Run away. Her bed hasn't been slept in. I found out just a few minutes ago when I went up to see why she hadn't come down. She's left a note.'

'A note! What does it say, Mrs Bunce?'

'It says there's something she's got to do.'

'What sort of thing?'

'She doesn't say. But she does say,' continued Annabel's mother, a note of menacing accusation entering her tone, 'that there's nothing else left for her to do and that it's because of the tree in the Rec. It's you that wants to cut it down, isn't it? She says you're a vandal.'

Mrs Stringer felt hot.

'Are you going to inform the police, Mrs Bunce?'

There was a muffled and urgent conversation at the other end of the line.

'My husband thinks we ought to. Straight away.'

'Let me know if you hear anything, won't you? Immediately.'

Mrs Stringer put the phone down in considerable alarm.

Mr Bunce, meanwhile, was studying Annabel's note more closely. He had been affected by his wife's near-panic when she had first come rushing downstairs but now he was cooling down. The note read:

Dear Mum and Dad,
Please don't worry about me but there is something I've got to do. I've been left with no other way. I can't tell you any more just now, only that it's about the tree in the Rec. The town council are a lot of vandals.

There were love and kisses from Annabel.

'On second thoughts,' he said, 'I'll ring Kate first.'

Kate had been expecting the call, not sharing Annabel's confidence that her parents would read the note and merely continue with breakfast.

'It's all right, Mr Bunce,' she said. 'I know where she is.'

There was a sigh of relief.

'Where, Kate?'

Kate had been fearing the question. She had been instructed by Annabel to answer only if there were no getting out of it but she'd known there wouldn't be. She told him and listened patiently to the exclamations of astonishment.

'But Mr Bunce, Annabel said I was to tell you it's

very important you don't tell anybody or try to see her.'

'We'll see about that.'

Afterwards, Kate went to see her own mother and told her she'd like to spend the morning in Querminster looking round the shops. Her mother was surprised.

'I don't mind, but aren't you going to stay and watch Mrs Stringer on telly? Everybody else in Addendon is. It should be good for a laugh.'

But Kate wanted to be out of the way. She hoped that Mr and Mrs Bunce would do as Annabel wanted although in the long run it wouldn't make any difference to anything, but anyway that was out of her hands. The best thing she could do was disappear before anybody else, including her own family, started asking awkward questions. She took the next bus to Querminster.

Gazing out of the window at the passing countryside she tried to put Annabel out of her mind because there was nothing more she could do to help, but it was impossible. Apart from anything else, there were too many trees around. Everywhere one looked, trees, trees, trees. No, she simply couldn't free her mind of Annabel; of her gallant, hopeless action and the despair that had led her to it.

Mrs Stringer couldn't free her mind of Annabel either as she waited for the television company car to pick her up. Annabel Bunce had run away to do something desperate! After a sordid quarrel with her, Mrs Stringer! Presumably the police were starting their search!

And when the car pulled up outside the door there was still no word from the Bunces to say that she had been found.

*

There had been no word because Mr and Mrs Bunce had been having something of a row, Annabel's mother being surprisingly stubborn in arguing that they ought to comply with Annabel's wishes and do nothing. This was mainly because she wanted to spite Mrs Stringer with whom she was furious for having, in her opinion, created the situation.

Mr Bunce – who in the meantime had discovered that his thick sweater and waterproof over-trousers were missing – sympathized, particularly, as he agreed with Annabel about the tree, but he did feel, reluctantly, that as responsible citizens they had a duty to inform Mrs Stringer and the town council.

In the end Mr Bunce won but by the time he rang, Mrs Stringer had left home.

'If we must tell somebody,' said Mrs Bunce, still reluctant, 'I'd rather tell Mr Poynton-Green anyway. He can pass on the message.'

Mr Poynton-Green was also preparing for the television broadcast when his phone rang, though his role would be a minor one. Like other members of the town council he would simply be on hand if needed.

In response to Mr Bunce's inquiry as to whether he would be seeing Mrs Stringer he confirmed that he would; was, indeed, about to add that he could see her now, though the window. She was getting out of a television company car and bustling along his garden path in a curiously agitated manner.

Listening to Mr Bunce, however, and seeing the state Mrs Stringer was in, he changed his mind and allowed the doorbell to ring, merely saying: 'Thanks very much for letting me know. Yes. I'll pass it on to Mrs Stringer. I'll be seeing her any moment.'

Having put the telephone down he opened the door.

'I wonder,' said Mrs Stringer, 'if I might use your phone to ring the Bunces. It's rather alarming. Their daughter ran away from home last night saying she was going to do something desperate. They were just about to ring the police when I last spoke to them and I want to find out if there's any news yet.'

'There's no need to ring,' said Mr Poynton-Green. He sounded grave and Mrs Stringer's heart sank. 'I was speaking to Mr Bunce only moments ago.'

'Has she come back? Have the police any news?'

'I'm afraid not.'

And that was all he said. He was, after all, in a desperate situation, ready to snatch at any opportunity of diverting Mrs Stringer from the birdbath issue.

'Oh, dear!' whispered Mrs Stringer. 'Oh, dear!'

*

Kate was exploring the clothes shops of Querminster, planning a new wardrobe to try to forget about things. She didn't have quite Annabel's capacity for trying on every garment in the shop and leaving the stock in a discarded heap on the table before moving on dissatisfied, but she was having a reasonably good try.

There wasn't any point, she kept on insisting to herself, in worrying. Nevertheless, she couldn't help wondering what was happening to Annabel *now*.

There was also the television programme. That was secondary but it did seem a pity to miss it. Then, while strolling around the ground floor of a department store it occurred to her that she needn't. They had a radio and television department upstairs, didn't they? And the television sets would be switched on.

She looked at her watch. The programme had been on five minutes already. Even so, Kate didn't hurry. The programme was of small importance compared with Annabel and the tree.

Anyway, she knew what was going to feature in it and it couldn't be less interesting. She'd read about it in the *Advertiser*. It was to start with a general look at Addendon and then Mrs Stringer, accompanied by the cameras and some of the councillors, was to stroll along the Corton Compton Road, talking all the way, to the proposed birdbath site where she was to enlarge upon the birdbath issue.

Kate had seen enough of Mrs Stringer and the town council in recent days. Vandals! Annabel was right.

Stepping off the escalator at the second floor, then, Kate was in a listless frame of mind, ill-prepared for what was to confront her as she turned a corner into the radio and television department; a scene so strange, so bizarre, so surrealistic that it stopped her in her tracks.

A dozen Mrs Stringers, in glorious colour, were gesturing and mouthing silently at her from as many television screens.

And what *was* she doing? This wasn't the planned stroll round Addendon. She was standing in front of a tree and behind her, huddled beneath the tree like some down-at-heel chorus in a modern opera was an abject-looking band of people, a motley collection of men and women; tall and short, stout and thin, tousle-haired and balding, sober and wild-eyed, pompously suited and scruffily be-jeaned – why! Surely! Yes, it was the Addendon Town Council! That same town council which had looked so imperious when seated round a table! Caught for once pallid and blinking in the great outdoors away from its natural habitat, the Memorial Hall!

What *was* it doing under a tree? And suddenly Kate recognized the tree. It was the tree in the Rec! The old soldier, the sylvan Chelsea Pensioner, Annabel's ideal of rottenness. What on earth –?

Why was Mrs Stringer writhing and gesticulating so extravagantly? Now she was turning to the town council, hands spread pleadingly like a choirmistress inviting them to sing. Had the planned programme been scrapped in favour of a sing-song? Kate could see Mr Poynton-Green among the councillors, standing at the back and gazing at the ground as if trying to pretend he wasn't there. And now the camera was on Mr Cantrill. He was addressing the councillors. They were all raising their hands . . .

And Kate suddenly knew what was happening. The town council was taking a vote. They were holding an extraordinary meeting beneath the tree in the Rec and they had just carried a motion unanimously. With a lurch of the heart she realized that it could only be about one thing.

Kate didn't need the sound turned up, didn't even want it to be. Crude sound would somehow have spoiled the wonder of it all.

But wait – there was a disturbance. A new character was coming on stage. It was Mr Crick, the tree surgeon. A dozen Mr Cricks, all bewildered and carrying a dozen chain-saws. The camera panned for a moment to show the dozen vans in which he'd arrived. Here he was, come to cut the tree down as promised to find himself appearing on a television show with the town council massed beneath the tree. Who would not have been bewildered in such circumstances?

And now a dozen Mrs Stringers were holding up a dozen pudgy hands in front of his dozen faces and clearly telling him to desist.

'Go away, Crick,' she appeared to be screeching. 'Go and take your chain saw with you and never darken the entrance to our recreation ground again. Crick, you vile villain, you are not wanted here.'

It was all crystal clear to Kate while at the same time bewildering. The town council had just decided not to have the tree cut down, after all – and in the nick of time! Mr Crick was being duly sent packing.

But what had caused them to change their minds? Had Annabel managed to persuade them in some way? But then why on television? Above all, where was she? Still where Kate had believed her to be or –?

A youthful, dark-suited sales assistant with a crisp little moustache was strolling round, hands clasped behind his back, one eye on the television.

'That looks a load of old corn,' he said to Kate, as he passed her. 'What is it, some old melodrama?'

'It's the Addendon Town Council,' said Kate, *Live From Addendon*.' Mr Crick was skulking away, casting crazed glances back over his hunched shoulders and Mrs Stringer was turning to face the camera again, apparently about to make a speech. She clasped her hands.

'Addendon!' said the sales assistant, interestedly. He went over and turned a knob on one of the sets.

'– Annabel Bunce –' Mrs Stringer blasted out at full volume, making Kate jump, before he adjusted the sound to a reasonable level, 'Annabel Bunce, in case you have just come to a television set I repeat: this tree will not come down. Here on television, an extraordinary meeting of the Addendon Town Council has just unanimously decided that.'

A feebly ingratiating smile appeared on Mrs Stringer's face. She placed a plump hand on her heart.

'Annabel, wherever you are, please believe me. I never wanted this tree felled –' Mrs Stringer waved an emotional hand at the rotting old soldier behind her – 'none of us did. It was only a concern for others that persuaded us, the instinctive and – surely – commendable compassion which one feels whenever a question of child safety arises. But that's over now because we've changed our minds.

'We've done so because we want you back, Annabel. Your loving parents want you back. Addendon wants you back. We want you back so much that we've changed the content of this programme so as to make this appeal in the hope that you'll see it. Wherever you are, Annabel, you can return at once knowing that the tree you love is safe.'

There followed an emotional stillness broken only by the sound of a bit of dead branch sliding out of the tree and plopping comfortably on to the grass. A few dead leaves drifted amongst the councillors.

Then a doubtful voice from somewhere above said: 'You won't change your minds again, will you? Cross your hearts?'

'Cross my heart,' said Mrs Stringer, mechanically doing so with great energy. There was a murmur as other councillors began to do likewise before confusion set in and they all started peering upwards to see where the voice had come from.

'Then I'll come down,' it said.

The camera had already abandoned Mrs Stringer and gone climbing the tree. It settled on a stirring in the leaves some distance up from which emerged a leg, clad in over-large rolled-up oilskin trousers, to grope cautiously and somewhat fearfully for a foothold on a lower branch. A canvas bag, perhaps used for holding provisions, fell and almost hit Mrs Stringer in the eye.

Annabel, as requested, was coming back.

Live From Addendon faded out. Its time was up. It had been a memorable programme which was to win its young director praise for its immediacy and use of the fly-on-the-wall technique and lead to better things for him, directing decent programmes with proper budgets shown at times when people were watching.

*

'I wonder why Mr Poynton-Green didn't pass on the message to Mrs Stringer,' said Kate, later that day.

'Don't know,' said Annabel. 'Don't care. I'm just glad he didn't.'

She gurgled her drink contentedly through the straw. They were strolling through Addendon, Annabel enjoying a regal progress as people, particularly Lord Willoughby's pupils, stopped to congratulate her on her television performance or shouted 'welcome back' to her from across the street.

'I would, though,' said Annabel, defiantly, 'have stayed up the tree till they got me down. I expect they'd have had to get the fire brigade out.'

It had been Annabel's despairing plan to sit up the tree until Mr Crick arrived with his chain-saw, then reveal herself and refuse to come down. In order to ensure secrecy until the last moment she'd sat up half the night, sneaking out before dawn in warm clothes and with a bag of provisions, to climb the tree before anyone was about and find a nice hidey-hole among the branches in which to rest. She'd had to get there early anyway because there was no telling what time Mr Crick might arrive.

It *had* been desperate, though. It could only have been a delaying action.

'There's Mr Poynton-Green now,' said Kate.

He was sauntering by on the other side of the road, swinging a stick, his old urbane self. Seeing them he raised his hat in a genial, pleasantly old-world manner. He was feeling warmly towards them this afternoon for a great weight had been lifted from his mind. The birdbath issue was dead.

He had no pangs of guilt about having played upon Mrs Stringer's fears and encouraged her to make her appeal on television. His view was that the television broadcast had been bound to be a fiasco with the town council revealed as idiots in some way or other. So they may as well look idiots over the rotting tree issue as the birdbath issue; better, in fact, because the birdbath issue would have exposed their idiocy over a period of years whereas the rotting tree issue was merely a one-off.

Besides, they would now be able to continue in the old happy ways, fighting and feuding. It would have spoilt it for them to learn that most of their previous fighting and feuding, since he had been Clerk, had been a waste of time. Yes, it was a very happy outcome.

Annabel and Kate paused by the Rec.

'They didn't get round to saying anything about

the birdbath, after all, did they,' said Kate. 'I suppose they'll just put it in the Rec now.'

'I'm glad about that,' said Annabel. Some of the old campaigning fires flickered hotly for a moment. 'I never did like the idea of the birds having to bathe with a lot of nosey people sitting watching them. I think they'll get more privacy in the Rec.'

From Annabel's point of view, too, it was a very happy outcome all round.

'Look, Annabel!' said Kate, 'There's your tree. I shall always think of it as your tree now.'

'I,' said Annabel, 'shall always think of it as Mrs Stringer's tree.'

'Oh, Annabel, that's a lot of rot.' Kate was indignant. 'It's yours. You were so brave climbing up there to save it. I'd never have dared.'

'A lot of rot! Kate, you are funny! Oh, Kate, I'm so glad I've got a witty friend!'

They went off, feeling so pleased with and proud of each other.